Lus

X Rated titles from *X Libris*:

Game of Masks	Roxanne Morgan
Acting It Out	Vanessa Davies
Private Act	Zara Devereux
Who Dares Sins	Roxanne Morgan
The Dominatrix	Emma Allan
House of Decadence	Lucia Cubelli
Sinner Takes All	Roxanne Morgan
Haven of Obedience	Marina Anderson
Secret Fantasy	Vanessa Davies
Degrees of Desire	Roxanne Morgan
Wicked Ways	Zara Devereux
Bound for Paradise	Ginnie Bond

Other titles in the *X Libris* series:

Arousing Anna	Nina Sheridan
The Women's Club	Vanessa Davies
Velvet Touch	Zara Devereux
The Gambler	Tallulah Sharpe
Forbidden Desires	Marina Anderson
Letting Go	Cathy Hunter
Two Women	Emma Allan
Pleasure Bound	Susan Swann
Silken Bonds	Zara Devereux
Rough Trade	Emma Allan
Cirque Erotique	Mikki Leone
Lessons in Lust	Emma Allan
Lottery Lovers	Vanessa Davies
Overexposed	Ginnie Bond
G-Strings	Stephanie Ash
Black Stockings	Emma Allan
Perfect Partners	Natalie Blake
Legacy of Desire	Marina Anderson
Searching for Sex	Emma Allan
Private Parties	Stephanie Ash
Sin and Seduction	Emma Allan
Island of Desire	Zara Devereux
Hotel of Love	Dorothy Starr
Teaching the Temptress	Ginnie Bond
Fanning the Fantasy	Zara Devereux

Lust Under Leo

Maria Lyonesse

X LIBRIS

www.xratedbooks.co.uk

An *X Libris* Book

First published in Great Britain in 2002
by X Libris

Copyright © Maria Lyonesse 2002

The moral right of the author has been asserted.

*All characters in this publication are
fictitious and any resemblance to real
persons, living or dead, is purely coincidental.*

All rights reserved.
No part of this publication may be reproduced,
stored in a retrieval system, or transmitted, in
any form or by any means, without the prior
permission in writing of the publisher, nor be
otherwise circulated in any form of binding or
cover other than that in which it is published and
without a similar condition including this condition
being imposed on the subsequent purchaser.

A CIP catalogue record for this book
is available from the British Library.

ISBN 0 7515 3289 4

Typeset by
Derek Doyle & Associates, Liverpool
Printed and bound in Great Britain by
Clays Ltd, St Ives plc

X Libris
An imprint of
Time Warner Books UK
Brettenham House
Lancaster Place
London WC2E 7EN

Lust Under Leo.

Chapter One

'*DO YOU KNOW* something?' Nick murmured as he trailed a moist fingertip along the outer curve of her breast. 'When my accountants come in here first thing tomorrow morning and remind me how predictably well the company's doing, I'll be sitting behind this very desk, thinking about what I did to my thoroughly edible marketing manager over it and getting one almighty hard on.'

Poised above him, her breasts dangling provocatively over his chest, Jenna giggled. She was getting aroused again. She loved the thought of Nick's sober business suit – that was now scattered on the boardroom floor around them – straining under an erection and all because of her. This feeling of power was turning her on.

Nick ran his hand down her back again, skimmed it over her buttocks and dipped his fingers into the warmth between her moist vaginal lips. Then round and round her pouting nipple he teased the slipperiness, coaxing what had once been satisfaction into a rising hunger for more. Jenna moaned and jiggled her breasts in his face. They both knew what it was doing to her. She'd thought this was going to be just one quick fuck in a snatched few minutes after work. Now she rolled the thought luxuriously around inside her head that soon she was going to feel Nick thrusting into her a second time.

Abruptly he stopped. 'So what about my invitation? Have you decided yet?'

'Sorry, what?'

'My birthday bash the weekend after next. Go on, say you'll be there. I know it's one of our own hotels but I've contracted out all the catering and entertainments. Well, Lisette has. There won't be anything to do except enjoy ourselves.'

'Won't Lisette be there too?'

'She's my wife – of course she will. But so what? The hotel's a big place.'

He began stroking the very tips of her nipples lightly again – enough to stir her hunger, not enough to take her further. God, why was Nick always like that? Playing her like a virtuoso. Even if she was on top, like she was now, he was the one in control. But she loved it. She never thought she would but, Christ, it turned her on.

'You know the place,' he continued, 'Netherdean Hall. That old manor house – Forest of Dean way. Don't say you've forgotten when we acquired it.' He winked. 'Big enough to get away from Lisette for a few hours here and there.'

He paused again, cupped her breast and drew her nipple fully into his mouth. It was still slick with the sweet taste of her juices, which he had massaged into it moments earlier. He closed his eyes and moaned like a man given something luscious to eat.

Then he drew his head away abruptly again. He

grinned at the sight of her nipple peaking out petulantly towards him. Lazily he gave it a flick with the tip of his tongue. Jenna groaned. She just wanted him to stop talking and penetrate her again.

'Come on,' he murmured, 'we'll have plenty of time to make these,' he kissed each of her breasts in turn, 'and this,' he dipped a finger between her slippery labia, 'very happy indeed.'

'Nick, I'm not sure, I—'

'Jenna, I need you there.' His voice had suddenly gone hard. 'It's not just friends. There'll be important business contacts, too. You're my right-hand woman. I need you.'

'Business. You never pass up an opportunity, do you?'

'Of course not.' He seemed to relax; her tone had been more admiring than accusatory. 'How else d'you think I got to head up a major European hotel and leisure group by the age of twenty-nine?'

By marrying a woman ten years older than yourself so you could get your hands on it, she wanted to reply – but didn't.

'It'll be a laugh,' he continued confidently, more sure of her agreement now. 'Everyone's got to wear historical fancy dress for the evenings.'

'What?'

'Only fair. I mean, not only is it a beautiful old building but surely me turning thirty is a pretty historic occasion. What could you be? Hmm, let's think . . .'

'Nick, I haven't said—'

'Lady Godiva,' he decided playfully. 'Riding in on a white horse with nothing to cover your eminently fuckable nakedness but hair.'

He began pulling her hair from its clips and arranging it down over her body. He picked out individual curls and trailed them round and round her dark areolae, deliberately missing the most sensitive tips. She shivered at the strange, ticklish sensation and her breasts swayed in front of his face. His grin widened at the sight.

'No, on second thoughts that would never work,' he said. 'You haven't got nearly enough hair to cover a gorgeous pair like those. What about. . . ?'

Jenna felt movement between her thighs. She rolled off Nick's body on to the boardroom table and glanced down. Whatever fantasy Nick was having was obviously taking effect. His cock was rising and stiffening against his thigh. She watched, fascinated. She loved the way it moved and swelled of its own accord. A beautiful, willing plaything. She didn't think she'd ever get tired of watching it, stroking it, taking it between her lips.

'Nell Gwyn,' he began again. 'Course, you'd have to have a really low-cut bodice and a corset that trussed you up just so . . .'

He placed one hand on the outer curve of each generous breast and moulded them tightly into a deep, thrusting cleavage.

'And a pile of oranges in your basket,' he continued, 'a really big pile. But as the night went on I'd take them away, one by one, until everyone in the room could see your luscious breasts – but not all of them, not quite all. Enough, though, that every man in the place would have a raging hard on. And I'd think, "Yeah, suckers, you might all want to but I'm the only man who's going to get to do this." '

Suddenly he dived on to her left breast and took as

much of it as possible into his mouth. His rough tongue snaked round her nipple, showing no mercy. Where a moment ago he had been calculating, keeping her dangling on a line, now he was all joyful, animal lust. Jenna gasped. She didn't want teasing or treating like a china doll. She wanted this: the healthy, robust appetite of an undeniably virile man.

'Oh Nick, please . . .'

She slipped her hand down without looking and found his thick shaft. It was fully erect now. She ran her fingers along its considerable length. They tingled as they enjoyed its texture – firm, velvety, always warm and willing for her. She couldn't help thinking, every time, what a beautiful cock Nick had. Apart from the satisfaction it could give her when it plunged deep into her body it was, simply, aesthetically perfect.

'Fuck me,' she whispered. 'Please, he's ready. So am I. Fuck me deep and hard like last time.'

Her fingertips moulded themselves over the foreskin and bulging glans. As if agreeing with her, his cock twitched and an impatient slipperiness began to cover her fingers. She rubbed this in, concentrating on the tender ridge just behind the glans. His cock was trembling now and she could feel the blood rushing through it. But Nick had other ideas.

He drew away from her and stood up. 'Jenna, you know the rules. You mustn't milk me dry. If I have trouble getting it up for Lisette tonight, she'll know something's going on. She's off to the Paris office tomorrow and she'll be there for the rest of this week and next. She'll expect it before she goes.'

She propped herself up on her elbows and looked at him. The sight of him standing there, his quivering erection pointing straight at her, was overpowering. Long and heavy as Nick's penis was, it stood as high as any adolescent boy's. She didn't believe his excuse for a moment.

'And she doesn't turn me on as much as you do, Jenna. You know that. I have to be really, really horny to give a passable performance for her. I mean, she might have big tits but believe me they've sagged. And she's nowhere near as sweet and tight as you.'

He reached over and drew a forefinger lazily between her labia and up around her swollen clitoris. She parted her legs willingly for him to carry on.

'Besides,' he continued mischievously, 'you haven't been a good girl. You haven't said "yes".'

'All right, Nick, all right. I'll do what you want, just . . .'

'Just what?'

'Just let me feel him in me, please.'

Nick grinned in triumph and seized the backs of her knees, hauling her towards him until her hips were level with the edge of the desk. He parted her thighs wide. Jenna felt absurdly helpless in this position. Her vulnerability excited her, too.

Still standing, Nick took his cock in one hand and stroked it slowly up and down the lips of Jenna's quim. She moaned and felt the hot trail of moisture flow faster from her and trickle down on to the expensively polished table top. Nick smiled and pushed his cock deeper between her welcoming lips, stretching her vagina and filling it to its hungriest depths. Jenna sighed with pleasure as she felt the bulbous head push all the way up inside her. She held her breath, waiting for the equally delicious sensation as it drew back again, almost to her outer lips then surged forwards once more. It didn't happen. Something was wrong.

Nick seemed content to wait there, his cock engulfed by her. Slowly he bent his hands and lips to her breasts, moulding and fondling them as he sucked desperately first one nipple, then the other. Jenna tossed her head from side to side and whimpered. She was proud of her full, firm breasts and the effect they'd had on lovers in the past. It turned her on, almost more than anything else, to have their exquisitely sensitive nipples sucked as thoroughly and single-mindedly as this. But their effect on Nick was something else altogether. She knew very well they aroused him so much he could probably reach orgasm just by this alone. He was cheating her.

She wouldn't let it happen. She bucked and gyrated her hips, trying to get enough leverage, enough friction against her clitoris so she could come before him, so she could win. She was so, so close. But Nick knew what he was doing. In that position, sprawled back against the desk, her helplessness wasn't just symbolic. It was very, very real. How many other women had he fucked like this before he'd got the balance absolutely right?

The more she struggled to get just the tiniest movement against his cock, the more insistent his hands and tongue on her breasts became. It was turning her on but it was turning Nick on even more. She was furious with him. Automatically her stomach muscles clenched but with them, too, the tight band of muscles encircling her vagina. She could tell by Nick's sudden gasp that this was a source of pleasure he hadn't dared anticipate.

She knew him well enough; she knew the signs.

Over the eighteen months they'd been lovers his cock had come inside her more times than she could begin to recall. Now it was still – not thrusting into her – she felt its kick more forcefully than ever. The moment of his climax was always wonderful for her – a bursting, stretching feeling filling her with warmth. This time it wasn't enough.

'You bastard,' she said as he opened his eyes. She said it without true feeling, though. He might still take pity on her. He might still bend down between her parted thighs and run his firm tongue in circles round her clitoris, lapping her eagerly to the orgasm she craved. He was good at it. He was good at anything involving sex – or money, too, come to that – and he knew it. But he kept her wanting. For all the times – in expensive hotel rooms, in his office between meetings, in his car parked up in the woods on remote 'fact-finding' trips – she'd willingly taken his splendid cock in her mouth and sucked and sucked until it exploded on her tongue, he'd gone down on her perhaps four or five times. And she didn't think he was about to increase that score.

Nick withdrew from her in one slick movement and began to pick up his clothes.

'You bastard,' she repeated with more feeling.

'First law of business, Jenna. Always leave them hungry for a little more. How else can I make sure you'll come away with me?'

'I said I would, didn't I?'

'Sort of. But can I be sure you meant it? And you also said, "Just let me feel him in me." ' He looked up and met her eyes. 'Just taking you at your word.'

'God, you can be infuriating sometimes!'

'I know.' He leant over and kissed her. 'I practise.

But I also know if you want me to make it up to you, you'll come to the party next weekend. And you do want me to. So you will.'

The late July sunlight that reflected off the road almost blinded her. With relief, Jenna turned off at the sign that said Netherdean Hall and underneath, in more discreet lettering, A Division of Treganza Leisure International. The long gravel drive crackled under her tyres for several minutes before she reached the lake. Oh yes, the bloody lake. Nick had pestered her more than once about restoring the lake to its former glory. She must arrange for it to be dredged out and turned into the sort of trout fishing attraction the Americans and Japanese loved. She'd faxed off a memo but it seemed to have been ignored. Was it really part of her remit as marketing manager to chase it up?

But she grinned to herself as she drove under the folly arch of the main entrance, her weekend party mood restored. Yes, she remembered their first trip out here when they were only toying with the idea of adding the rambling sixteenth-century manor with its extensive wooded grounds to the group. Nick, sitting casually at a table in what was now the breakfast room, trying to keep a straight face during talks with the previous owner while, underneath the table, Jenna slipped off one shoe, ran her stockinged foot up Nick's leg and nestled her big toe between his thighs. She'd hidden her smile behind a coffee cup. He'd tried to look non-committal while her sheer stocking rubbed fluidly up and down over the outline of his erection which was becoming more and more distinct by the second.

And afterwards he'd spun the wheels of his Toyota Land Cruiser on the gravel drive in his haste to get away. In between gear changes his left hand had strayed from the wheel, inched up her skirt and found the wetness between her thighs. His fingers had bored quickly into her, arousing her and – she'd glanced briefly over to where a promising bulge was reappearing in his lap – arousing him, too.

It had been winter. It was already getting dark. At the first opportunity Nick had pulled over into a tiny lane and bundled her into the back seat. Her face had been pressed against the leather upholstery. She'd breathed in its decadent scent. Removing the very minimum of clothing he'd mounted her roughly from behind, thrusting without mercy. The novelty, the recklessness of it had burned her into a raw, sweet orgasm that had carried on glowing between her legs all the way back to London. They'd been lovers for less than a fortnight, then. Even so, Jenna had known it wasn't just the boldness of her snaking foot beneath the table that had aroused him out of control. Nick was never so horny as when closing a deal.

Now they were back. She wondered, why here? Nick could be absurdly sentimental, though he'd rather die than admit it. Nevertheless, as she drew into the car park she felt the pleasant buzz of blood rushing to her clitoris as the memory of that last time stirred her senses. She and Nick hadn't made love since that evening in the boardroom – frustrating but oh, what a supreme example of how well he knew how to whet her appetite. Her clitoris thumped again as she imagined him 'making it up' to her.

But Nick's powerful Land Cruiser wasn't among the few cars in the car park. Neither was Lisette's yellow sports car come to that. Disappointed – but not too much, as she'd been deliberately early to miss the worst of the Friday traffic – Jenna got out of the car and began to lift her weekend bag from the boot.

'You're not in costume.'

She whipped round at the voice. For a moment she'd thought it was Nick's but the man standing in front of her was nothing like her outwardly conventional lover. He had longer hair and a dark, close-clipped beard. His body tended to slender and wiry rather than Nick's natural stockiness honed at his private gym. He was dressed – how could she best put it? – like a barbarian. There was a heavy silver torque around his neck. And then she jumped back suddenly. The snake on his left arm opened its eyes and hissed. She hadn't expected it to be real.

A second later the scent hit her. It was a subtle thing; it seemed to emanate from him. You had to be standing very close to notice it at all. Close enough to feel his body heat over the heat of the day. It was something like musk, something like crushed leaves, but undeniably, eminently masculine. It crept into her personal space, disarming her.

'Well,' she replied eventually, 'I'd get a few funny looks driving down from London dressed as an Elizabethan tavern wench. You seem to have a head start on the rest of us, though. Who are you supposed to be?'

'Cernunnos.'

'Who?'

'Cernunnos. Sure, everyone's heard of the Greek god Pan, but Cernunnos is the home-grown version. The Celtic lord of the animals.' He lifted his arm again; it hissed. 'Hence the snake. Oh, don't look like that – Lilith won't hurt you. She's only a baby boa constrictor. Lilith the second, I should say.'

She plucked up the courage to stroke the snake's patterned back. It was surprisingly dry to the touch and warm.

'That's better,' he commented. 'I'm always suspicious of people who can't cope with snakes. They're a symbol of unrepressed sexuality, you know. As is Cernunnos.'

She looked up at him sharply. She got the feeling she was being challenged. And she couldn't work out quite how she felt about it.

'Are you one of Nick's business associates?' she demanded. 'I don't recognise you.'

He chuckled at the thought. 'No. I'm the entertainments manager for the weekend – my job is to make sure everyone gets to relax and have a good time. Freelance, of course.' He winked. 'You can call me Robin. And you are. . . ?'

'Jenna Mills,' she replied stiffly. 'Marketing manager at Treganza Leisure International.'

'Ah, in that case this'll be your room key,' he said, producing something from his pocket and dangling it in front of her.

'Which you just happened to have on you,' she said as she snatched it.

'Let's just say I had certain information. First left at the top of the staircase. Enjoy.'

Jenna carried her bags up the long, gloomy staircase. Her room, in contrast, was bright and overlooked lawns that swept down to the lake and the beginnings of the wood. More importantly, it had an en suite bathroom. She took a shower while waiting for Nick.

As she stood under the warm cascade, the crushed-leaves scent came back to haunt her. Subtle as it was, it seemed to reach her through the exotic, perfumed soap. Under its influence a creamy feeling rose in her lower belly. She began soaping her breasts, rejoicing in their slipperiness and imagining it wasn't her own hands but a lover's doing this to her. The spicy, heady scent had taken her over, made her its own. A diffuse sensuality tingled through her body. She was very, very ready for Nick to come and take her. Or, a small but seditious thought told her, it didn't have to be Nick.

Jenna stepped out of the shower and dried herself. She unpacked her fancy dress costume and hung it in the steam for the creases to drop out. Elizabethan was what she'd finally managed to get – from a theatrical hire place just round the corner from the office. If she knew Nick, though, she could bet on his approval.

'I want you to look stunning,' he'd said to her a few days before. 'There are going to be some people you really need to have eating out of your hand. You've got it, babe. Use it.'

The dress was very low cut. The lace-up bodice pushed her breasts up high and forwards as if the slightest breath would dislodge the flimsy material that teetered precariously just above her nipples and leave her bare for everyone to see. Her hands strayed automatically to the upper curves of her breasts as she remembered how it had felt – how full and voluptuous they'd looked when she'd first tried the bodice on. She'd often dressed that way for lovers – worn basques and push-up bras and loved the way it made her feel. Now, though, a room full of men, many of them strangers, were going to be staring at those generous, upthrust curves. The wantonness of it excited her. Moving her hands down to her labia and dipping one forefinger between them she found they were unsurprisingly soft and moist.

To start with, though, a modern concession. She fastened a black suspender belt around her narrow waist and began rolling sheer, silky stockings up her legs. As she clipped the last suspender into place there was a knock on the door.

'Who is it?' she called.

'It's me.'

Jenna was none the wiser. It sounded like Nick. But then, so did the man who'd called himself Robin.

Just in case, she snatched up the towel from the bed and wrapped it around her.

'Come in,' she replied. 'It's open.'

Nick grinned wolfishly as he shut the door behind him. 'What's with the cover up? Gone all shy all of a sudden?'

'Nick, I wasn't sure if it was—'

He cut her off with a deep kiss, his tongue thrusting into her as uncompromisingly as his cock had done so many times. His right hand glided up her silky thigh and began to play with the deep lace trim that edged her stockings.

'I always knew you were a stockings and suspenders woman,' he murmured in her ear, 'right from the day I interviewed you. I had a bet with myself. I remember sitting opposite you, looking at those fabulous legs so coolly crossed and imagining what it would be like to run my fingers right up here. And I was thinking, God, I hope I don't have to move this wad of interview notes from my lap. She'll see what a massive hard on I've got for her.'

Jenna giggled. She knew this game of Nick's by now. Recalling erotic interludes out loud was one of his favourite ways of turning himself on. Did this mean, she wondered, they might have an hour or two together before Lisette showed up? She licked her lips and couldn't wait to see what happened when he moved his probing fingertips up further and found that stockings and suspenders were all she'd had time to put on and that her other lips were just as moist and glistening.

'So, babe. What do you reckon to the place?' he asked. 'You can live on champagne and asparagus all weekend if you like.'

'As I remember, something meatier was supposed to be on offer. Where's Lisette?'

He shrugged. 'You know she was due to fly back from Paris this morning. So anywhere between here and Heathrow, I guess.'

'Nick! But she could be—'

'Could be here any minute. Yeah. But she'll hardly come looking for us in here.' He ran his fingers up the back of her thigh and began stroking the soft skin on her buttocks. It was warm from her shower and still a little damp. 'Doesn't the threat of it turn you on, anyway? Let's see if it does . . .'

He moved his hand round between her thighs, joyfully discovering she wasn't wearing anything else. He parted her labia with one fingertip. She sighed and felt a letting go as more slipperiness trickled out over his hand.

'God, Jenna, you're one horny bitch,' he muttered.

He snaked a forefinger deep into her quim and wriggled it. She moaned as it touched her G-spot, sending shivers of pleasure up and down the eager length of her vagina. His middle finger eased in to join the first. He parted them, stretching her as he knew she loved being stretched. She clamped her muscles against them and squeezed. Nick smiled approvingly. She knew the unusual strength of her vaginal muscles. She was proud of them. It could drive her lovers wild.

'And that's what I'd like to do to your cock,' she whispered.

Nick pulled away from her, taking her towel with him and tossing it aside. He lay back on the bed, his hands folded behind his neck. He was still fully clothed. He hadn't even taken off his jacket. She was bare breasted and nothing but tufts of pubic hair were covering the darkening, pouting lips beneath.

'Let me look at you,' he insisted. 'Show yourself to me.'

She knew this game, too. Other lovers she'd enjoyed but Nick turned sex into something else altogether. His ready desire and easily coaxed erection could mean explosive sex at any snatched moment but it was these drawn-out games where his appetite really came into its own. He played with her frustration, drew it out until her hunger was greater than she could ever have imagined. He infuriated her. He also thrilled her more than any other man had ever done.

Yet all the while the thought nudged the back of her mind that this could all be just another elaborate tease. At any moment the yellow sports car might speed up the drive and Nick would be gone to meet his wife, greeting Lisette lovingly, making her a gift of his proud erection and leaving Jenna aching with lust. Jenna felt an unaccustomed stab of jealousy. She had created that desire. Only she should feel it plunge between her thighs.

'Let me look at you,' he repeated. 'Let me look at your best jewel.'

Obediently she placed one foot up on the bed, her thighs parted wide. Her vagina was glistening with its own readiness, her inner lips parting for him as they darkened and swelled. She wanted nothing more than to welcome him in – that most beautiful part of him, his warm, pulsating cock. With her legs stretched wide to display herself, even the partial release of pressing her thighs together to stave off that craving was denied her. Nick looked up and smiled.

'Do you know why a woman in stockings and suspenders is so sexy?' he murmured. 'It frames you. You're dressed in something but at the same time you're naked. It draws the eye to the most important part. It's hard black lines against ruby red softness. It looks like you're offering yourself as something delicious to eat.'

With that he sat up and flicked the very tip of his tongue lazily up and down against her exposed clitoris. The sensation was too intense. She wanted the longing to build up and up almost to more sweetness than she could bear before she finally came. She moaned and shifted just out of his reach.

Nick followed her and dipped his tongue further back into the honeypot between her pouting lips. Lazily he ran it backwards and forwards in her smoothness, lapping at her juices greedily like a cat with the freshest cream. This sent slow, billowing waves of pleasure up through her vagina. This, she knew and Nick knew, was how she loved to be played.

Suddenly he lay back on the bed again, his arms flung upwards as if in surrender. Though cheated at the abrupt withdrawal of his skilful tongue, she enjoyed the sight of him below her. His erection strained the expensive fabric of his trousers like a tent pole. She guessed its freedom to move meant he was wearing boxers underneath. She guessed it wouldn't be much longer now before she was allowed to know.

'Prowl on me, baby,' he muttered throatily. 'Make me so horny for you it hurts.'

She crouched on all fours astride him on the bed, very gradually working her way up his body. Her heavy breasts were swinging freely as she crawled. Her nipples grazed the legs of his trousers. The slightly scratchy fabric made them buzz with longing but soon she wanted more. She prowled further up his body, dragging her breasts over the buckle and heavily embossed leather of his designer belt. The contrast in textures and the sudden coldness of the metal hardened her nipples into peaks.

And then she caught the scent again. The musky scent that invaded her, penetrating deep into her lungs and making her realise, abruptly, how even breathing could be an erotic act. The question flashed into her mind without her knowing why she wanted to ask it.

'Nick, who's Rob—'

His mobile phone rang.

Cursing, Jenna rolled off him and flopped by his side on the bed. Nick reached into an inside jacket pocket and took out the phone. Her heart thundered, as did her frustrated vagina, as she lay there stiffly and listened to one side of the conversation.

'Huh . . . yeah, sure . . . when? . . . Okay, see you then . . . Look forward to it . . . Missed you, too, baby.'

He broke the connection, rolled over and grinned at her. 'That was Lisette in case you hadn't guessed. Her flight was delayed. She's on her way from Heathrow now but she's running late. You needn't be listening for footsteps in the hall for at least two hours, I reckon. So what are you going to do with me?'

He'd taken off his jacket and shrugged it aside. Already his fingers were busy unbuttoning his shirt. Jenna's mind was on more promising things. Because she knew he enjoyed it, she undid his belt buckle with her teeth. Likewise the clasp on his trousers and his zip. As Nick stripped off his other clothes she nuzzled her way through to feel the silk of his boxer shorts against her cheek. She rubbed her face against the shape of his erection and drank in a deep breath of his masculine scent. Then she probed through the slit in his shorts to breathe tantalisingly on his cock.

Under her breath and, increasingly, her lips and tongue it stirred and strained towards her. She slipped his trousers and shorts over his hips and freed his cock to take it fully into her mouth. She loved to suck it. When the bulbous tip filled her mouth and the veins in the shaft pulsed against her stretched lips, pumping in more and more blood, she sometimes felt her mouth was going to have an orgasm in sympathy. But this afternoon she had other ideas for his swollen cock and, obviously, so did he. As soon as he was completely naked, Nick withdrew from her, pushed her face down on to the quilt and twisted over to straddle her from behind.

He tucked his hands under her hips and raised them up towards him, spreading her buttocks wide. In this position the suspender straps cut deeply into her from behind but it wasn't unpleasant – far from it. It focused all her attention on the agreeable stretching sensation she was feeling in the cleft of her ass.

She felt Nick's cock run lazily up and down that cleft. She felt the trickle of impatient fluid seeping from its head. He began to rub it into her stretched skin, letting his cock linger suggestively as he circled it round and round her tight asshole. It felt deliciously taboo. Many times she'd wondered about being penetrated there but Nick's cock was too thick for such a tight opening. Still, it didn't stop her imagining. She was sure he was going to take her from behind this time and in such a position just fantasising about the so-close but illicit alternative brought her closer and closer to the brink.

Nick's fingers found the inviting wetness of her quim. They weren't gentle. By now she didn't want them to be. He made sure she was parted and moist enough for him, then positioned his cock head precisely and plunged in deep.

She gasped as he began to thrust. Too many men were tentative at this point. Not Nick. One of the things about him that obsessed her was his sureness, his firmness, his ability to thrust like this as long as necessary, penetrating her more fully than any lover had done before.

His hands slipped forwards from her hips and raised her up on to all fours. While thrusting energetically from behind he fondled her breasts and rolled and pinched her nipples just as greedily. Her face-down position lent her breasts more weight – made them seem even bigger than before. She knew this turned him on. His unashamed response to them turned her on, too – a simple, lusty appreciation of her womanhood.

Her clitoris was pouting, aching to be rubbed. Nick was moulding her prominent nipples between his thumb and forefinger, totally absorbed in this pleasure. She knew he wouldn't give up even one handful to move down lower and fondle the neglected bud. She longed to do it herself. But she couldn't possibly support his weight and hers on one hand alone.

But Nick had altered his angle of thrusting. Now the tip of his cock was stroking the front of her vagina, massaging that mythical G-spot many doubted the existence of but Jenna knew was definitely there. It didn't matter about her unrubbed clitoris now. The quick strokes of his cock against that tingling, sensitive spot were building up a warm wave in the tops of her thighs. Jenna moaned deeply. This way was so sweet, so leisurely. She knew it was going to happen. She didn't have to force anything.

The warm wave blossomed in intensity. It surged, filling her vagina with a sweet, almost aching fullness. Waves and waves followed it, clamping tight against Nick's cock as he relentlessly continued thrusting. She loved to feel him in her after she'd already come. Then, her vagina was at its most sensitive, most fully able to rejoice in the power and texture of his cock.

Nick was too experienced a lover not to realise this. For a few minutes longer he continued thrusting with the same, easy rhythm. Then, when he judged she'd had enough time to simply enjoy his cock, he pulled out further, thrust in deeper and she felt his shaft swell even bigger inside her and she clasped her muscles tight against him as he came.

She kept her muscles clenched like that to prevent him from withdrawing too soon. She loved that moment. It was like being balanced on a delicious knife edge, feeling so full of his cock and so satisfied but at the same time hungry for the next, stolen time when they'd be able to make love like this.

Slowly, still deeply coupled, they sank back down on to the bed. Playfully Nick twitched his cock a couple of times inside her. It shivered against the sensitive, still-pulsing tissues of her vagina. She wriggled her hips appreciatively as the little aftershocks of pleasure chased up and down from the swollen pink lips of her vulva to the very depths of her womb.

As Jenna rested her face against her hands, that musky scent took her by surprise yet again. She sniffed her fingers curiously. How had it lingered on her? Had she touched the man's arm, inadvertently, as she'd cautiously touched his snake?

She was about to question Nick again about Robin when she felt him begin to pull out of her. Then all her attention was focused on his bulbous glans retreating down the length of her vagina, caressing her flesh as it went. She rolled over and looked up at him. God, she thought, he was still impressive even after making love. That greedy cock took ages to go down.

'I'd better go,' he murmured apologetically. 'Don't be late for the pre-dinner drinks, will you? And do up the laces on that tavern wench corset as tight as they'll go. You're going to need to look good enough to eat. There's one guy in particular I really want you to impress.'

Chapter Two

JENNA PAUSED A MOMENT before she entered the large banqueting hall. She actually felt nervous. This was ridiculous. Here she was, a high-flying marketing executive and only twenty-eight. She was used to walking into rooms full of unknown people.

But this was different. When she went to work she was dressed in close-fitting and flattering but ultimately conventional business suits. Sure, men were reminded of her femininity by her abundant wavy hair and the generous swell of her breasts under her pale silky blouses. But her sexuality wasn't something she overtly played on.

Now, though, her waist was nipped in tightly and those breasts were thrust up on display for everyone to see. It made her feel vulnerable but at the same time that vulnerability gave her a low-level buzz of arousal. She couldn't hide behind the façade of the career woman – couldn't hide the self that kept saying, 'This is a party,' and wanted to be let off the leash to play. Still, if Nick thought she could do it . . .

She pushed open the door. As soon as Nick realised she'd arrived he grabbed her arm, drew her aside behind a large cheese plant and handed her the long glass of Pimms he had waiting for her.

'Now,' he said as she sipped, 'just a quick briefing. Who here don't you know?'

She tore her eyes away from him reluctantly. Nick was dressed as a Renaissance courtier – complete with ornate black and silver codpiece. There was something about codpieces. You just couldn't help looking.

Nevertheless, Jenna glanced across the room. Of course it was always difficult to recognise people in fancy dress, but the only familiar faces were Nick's wife Lisette and his drippy sister Heather. Lisette was picking at olives on the buffet table and looking bored. Her costume seemed eighteenth century and, like most of the women's, was low-cut. She still managed to look very chic and Parisian. She was attractive, of course, in the cool, self-assured way French women often are. Jenna couldn't imagine her rising to meet Nick's frankly animal desires.

'What's Lisette supposed to be?' Jenna asked. 'Heroine of the Bastille or something?'

'Yeah, something like that. Never mind about her, though. It's Alex I want you to impress. I'm not sure if he's . . .'

Nick's eyes narrowed and scanned the crowd. Jenna looked keenly, too. If she had to chat someone up on business, who would she most like it to be?

Her attention was caught by a highwayman in tight black leather trousers and thigh-length boots. His dark hair was caught in a ponytail at the nape of his neck. He looked as if he had a superbly athletic body. At the moment all his attention seemed to be focused on a very voluptuous and minimally dressed Cleopatra.

'Who's she?' Jenna asked.

'Cleopatra? She's Eleni. She's Greek and she's in textiles. Her firm supplied a lot of the brocades for the refurbishment of this place. Actually,' he smirked, 'she's an ex-lover of mine. Oh, from years ago. Before I was married.'

'You invited your ex-lover? How do I know you're not going to sneak off and refresh your memory?'

She'd meant it to sound like a joke. But it hadn't. Jealousy had introduced a tremor into her voice. That had been a mistake. Nick loved playing on people's vulnerabilities.

'Well, it's my birthday bash,' he murmured. 'I think I've got a right to indulge myself. Besides,' he lowered his voice, 'she's got the most mind-blowing cock-sucking technique I've ever met. If you don't keep me happy I might just have to renew my acquaintance with it.'

Nick was joking. Like she'd been joking. Wasn't he? Jenna drew a swift breath. Her trussed-up breasts strained against the precariously low-cut neckline of her bodice and the effect wasn't wasted on Nick. She had his attention again.

'So,' she countered quickly, 'is it the kinky highwayman I've got to jiggle these at? It would be a pleasure.'

'No,' Nick snapped fiercely. 'I don't want you moving in on him. And I think I'm going to have to break him and Eleni up soon.'

'No need to bite my head off.'

'Sorry. It's just ... Morgan Heselton is one of the top London choreographers.'

'And one of the few who isn't gay judging from the way he's looking at your ex.'

'I don't need reminding, thanks. He runs a modern

ballet troupe. My sister's training as a dancer. I want him to notice her.'

'The vestal virgin? She hasn't done herself many favours in the competition, Nick.'

Heather, Nick's sister, was loitering on the outskirts of the crowd. She was willowy, so much younger than Nick, and her costume, compared to most of the women's, looked demure.

It was like something an original Charleston dancer from the 1920s might have worn. It came from an era of high necklines and dropped sash waists, and it certainly wasn't figure-hugging. From the way the flounced skirt hung around Heather's long legs Jenna guessed the subtle 'ashes of roses' fabric might well be real silk taffeta. It was expensive. It was a work of art. But sexy? No.

'She's nothing like you,' Jenna murmured.

'She's my half sister. And I don't have time to give you the family history – not now.'

Jenna glanced back to Morgan and Eleni but noticed that now Robin had come on to the scene. Eleni turned her full attention to him, fascinated by the snake still coiled around his forearm.

The corner of Nick's mouth curled as he looked at the creature. 'Why do we have to have that bloody thing in here?'

'Threatened by snakes, Nick? Freud would have a field day.'

'I . . . I'll tell you about it some other time. That's him!'

'Sorry – who?'

For a moment Jenna was confused and didn't realise where he was pointing. She'd thought for a split second he was talking about Robin.

'There – pay attention, can't you? Alex Dumont – he's standing by the buffet table, talking to Lisette. Dressed as a Confederate general. God, can't the Americans be a bit more original for once? He owns a chain of leisure complexes in the States. There are one or two deals bubbling up in Europe at the moment that are too big for us to handle on our own. I'm hoping he might come on board as an investor.'

'So why is it me who's supposed to be softening him up?'

Nick looked back at her then glanced pointedly down at her cleavage. 'I'm not built for it like you are.'

'No, I mean why not Lisette? They seem to have plenty to chat about over there.'

Nick went quiet for a moment as if this was an option he hadn't considered – and she knew he hated being caught out like that.

'No,' he said finally. 'Lisette doesn't really know how to flirt. Oh, I know that being French it should come naturally to her, but I don't think it does. You'd make a better job of it.'

Jenna squinted again at Alex. Under the wide-brimmed army hat there seemed to be something not quite right. She couldn't figure it out from this distance.

'Does that mean you're expecting me to sleep with him?'

It was her turn to score a point in the jealousy stakes. Nick's wine glass snapped in his hand. He looked embarrassed and dumped the pieces in the heavy ceramic cheese-plant pot.

'Don't be stupid,' he hissed. 'You're a very intelligent woman. You know damn well how to play a man along. Be unattainable. Be his fantasy. Be the one he thinks about tonight when he climbs into bed and pulls his dick. But for God's sake don't be the one who messes this up for me. I mean it, Jenna. And listen, if you want a good conversation opener ask him how his marine centre is going. The one that's just opened in Florida. It's won loads of industry awards but act surprised when he tells you about them. Now come on. We've been out of things for far too long. Let's mingle. Separately.'

When Nick left Jenna and strode out across the room, he suddenly felt good about all of this. He'd left the first stage of things in her capable hands. Now he was going to relax and enjoy himself.

A waitress stopped and offered him a tray of drinks. He thought it was the same girl who'd served him earlier. Or maybe not. There were two of them buzzing around – both redheads, both dressed alike, so similar they might have been sisters or even twins.

Their costumes resembled Jenna's, but if anything were even tighter and more revealing. They both had the sort of creamy, plump, eminently touchable skin that natural redheads have. And a light dusting of freckles drew even more attention to the exaggerated upper curves of their breasts. They were the sort of girls, Nick thought, who naturally wore the label 'wench'. Whichever agency supplied these two seemed to know his tastes as well as he did himself.

As Nick chose another glass of wine from the tray, the girl lowered her eyelashes and smiled knowingly at him. His palms positively itched. He promised himself that before the weekend was out he was going to see what one or other of them looked like beneath those tight bodices. He deserved it.

For Nick was unashamedly and unreconstructedly a breast man. That was why his youthful adventures with the voluptuous Eleni were so sweet a memory. That was why finding out that his new and highly competent marketing manager was also highly beddable had been the icing on the cake. That was why, despite what he'd said to Jenna, sex with his wife was still a pleasure, although a little one-sided he felt at times.

Him and Lisette. He grinned and shook his head. No one else really understood why their relationship ticked. Certainly not Jenna. It worked because in many ways they were alike. Lisette, the dilettante photographer who'd married an older man for money. And had been left a rich widow with a reasonably successful hotel empire while still in her thirties. At which point a young and ambitious Nick had seduced then married her. She'd seen straight through him but she'd known he could make the company double or even treble in size. And he had done – and more. They were both mercenary. In a funny sort of way, they were soul mates.

Jenna eased her way through the crowd. She was very aware of the way her dress dictated her movements – it made her so intensely conscious of her woman's body. Jenna the new millennium career girl was slipping away. She really did feel like some Elizabethan tavern wench. Wench – she rolled the word around in her head and found she liked it. Fancy dress had been an inspired stroke of Nick's. They really were becoming other people. If one of the men, in passing, had casually slapped her on the behind she wouldn't have been remotely surprised. Or, indeed, offended.

Robin was standing close to the voluptuous Cleopatra-Eleni. As Jenna passed by he caught her eye and winked. She didn't acknowledge him. She wove on until she came to the buffet table where Alex and Lisette were still chatting.

Alex Dumont looked up suddenly, inclined his head and raised his wide-brimmed cavalry officer's hat.

'Evening, ma'am,' he said in a passable Southern drawl. 'I don't believe we've . . .'

As he raised his hat she saw he was completely bald, though he couldn't be more than mid-forties. She balked at this. Jenna liked a good head of hair on a man. Nick's for instance, which was dark, glossy and utterly touchable. She found herself filing this information about Alex away under 'Mildly disappointing: look for compensations'. His voice was like honey. And he had mischievous eyes which even now were holding her gaze a moment too long. Then she pulled herself up sharp. She was supposed to be inviting him into Treganza Leisure International – not her bed.

'Jenna Mills,' she said, extending her hand. 'I understand you're Alex Dumont.'

She had a firm, confident handshake. She knew she did. Some men found that disconcerting. Some men found it a challenge. But Alex did something none of them had ever done before. He took the proffered hand, raised it to his lips and kissed it slowly. Never did his gaze let go of hers. She hadn't expected it to feel so intimate.

'Sure, I've heard that name,' he replied. 'Aren't you the little lady Nick Treganza couldn't do without? Professionally, I mean.'

Jenna risked a sideways glance at Lisette. There

was no flicker of reaction on the cool, Parisian face. She was licking guacamole from raw vegetable crudités in a way that was both world weary and at the same time deeply sensuous. Only a French woman could manage that.

'I'm flattered,' Jenna said. 'I head up Nick's marketing team – the UK side, that is. I'm really just one part of a Europe-wide organisation.'

Keep the corporate flag flying, she told herself. Stress we're a major player in the field. Don't let yourself get too distracted by wondering what other old-fashioned charms might be lurking up that cavalry-uniformed sleeve.

She was poised to ask him about the Florida complex. But just as she opened her mouth he took the empty glass from her hand. She couldn't remember having finished it.

'Can I get you another, Jenna?'

'Oh, thank you. Pimms, please.'

'I'll have a dry white wine,' Lisette said, without turning and without having been asked.

Jenna watched Alex as he moved through the crowd in search of one or other of the red-haired waitresses. She found herself approving of the way he moved. There might well be compensations after all. Like her, he'd slipped easily into his part. She could well imagine him all day in the saddle, his lithe body keeping a natural rhythm with that of his horse. He looked remarkably fit.

Well, she thought, I suppose you don't own a chain of leisure resorts without trying them out yourself.

'You're here for pleasure, remember.' She heard Robin's voice beside her ear. 'You don't have to do everything he tells you.'

Jenna whipped round but he'd already gone.

And then there was that scent again, the scent that had lingered around her when she'd first met Robin that afternoon. Leafy, musky, green – if indeed a scent could have a colour.

Lisette must have noticed it too. She looked up and took a deep breath in, though she didn't remark on it directly. She looked properly at Jenna for the first time.

'Isn't it hot?' she said, trailing her fingertips along the neckline of her dress.

Jenna noticed a rosy flush beginning to appear in the hollow at the base of Lisette's throat. Nick had mentioned it to her, teasingly, once. He'd said it was a sign his wife was feeling really horny – not that that seemed to happen often enough as far as Nick was concerned.

'There's something strange about the air tonight,' Lisette continued distractedly. 'Strange . . .'

'You've noticed it, too? Perhaps Nick's been lacing the Pimms with Spanish Fly.'

'Him?' Lisette's voice returned to its clipped, pragmatic norm. 'He's far too mean. He wouldn't pay out more than he had to for his own party. It had to be in one of our own hotels. I wish he'd chosen one with a swimming pool. I'd love a swim.'

She was right, Jenna realised. The air had become so close and humid. The feeling of water on her body would have been just the thing.

'There's always the lake,' she found herself saying. 'They still haven't got round to dredging it out so it can't be more than four or five feet deep at most. We'd be perfectly safe.'

'I didn't bring any bathing things.'

'Me neither.' Jenna grinned. 'But so what?'

A sudden feeling of rebelliousness took her over. The last thing Nick wanted was for her to leave an important contact like Alex Dumont in the lurch. And surely the second last thing he wanted her to do was run off playing naughty schoolgirls with his wife. That seemed as good a reason as any to go for it.

'Come on,' she said, impulsively reaching for Lisette's hand. 'Don't tell me a French woman's too shy for a spot of skinny dipping.'

Lisette returned her clasp enthusiastically. They slipped round behind the buffet tables, through the French windows and down across the dark sloping lawn.

They stopped at the far side of the lake, beyond the reach of the floodlights that lit up the Hall's immediate grounds and in the welcoming shadows of the Victorian boathouse. Jenna began to pull at the laces of her bodice, but in her haste she pulled the wrong end and made the knot even tighter.

'Shit,' she muttered.

'Here, let me.'

Lisette stepped in and undid the laces with practised, efficient hands. When Jenna's bodice was lying on the grass she reached round behind her and undid the hidden zip at the back of the pale linen dress. She eased it down over Jenna's shoulders, all the while her lips curving in a cool smile that was utterly unreadable.

'Your hair looks different, Jenna,' Lisette murmured. 'You clip it back so practically for the office. It suits you more . . . natural.'

She reached up for a moment and twined a tawny curl of it between her fingers. Then the dress, too, slithered to the grass and Jenna's breasts were bare. Lisette held them for a moment in her elegant, long-fingered hands as if assessing them.

Jenna took a sharp breath in and her breasts swelled into Lisette's cupped palms. She'd never been in this situation before. She didn't quite know what it meant. Many male lovers had eagerly handled her breasts but never a woman. Was she about to be seduced by her lover's wife? There was something doubly licentious about that. It sent a shiver through her lower belly.

'Aren't you going to return the favour?' murmured Lisette. 'My dress isn't as complicated as yours – just hooks and eyes down the back.'

Jenna reached round to undo Lisette's dress. She had to press herself very closely into the other woman's arms. Lisette continued to fondle her breasts, rolling her nipples between thumb and forefinger. Jenna moaned with unexpected pleasure but Lisette stifled her moan as she covered the younger woman's mouth with a deep, penetrating kiss.

It seemed to take for ever to undo Lisette's dress – tiny hook by tiny hook. All the while Lisette's hands and Lisette's tongue were drawing muffled groans from Jenna's throat.

I can't believe I'm doing this, Jenna thought. I never imagined . . . I'm attracted to men. I love the sight and feel of their cocks. But this, with Lisette, it just feels right.

When Lisette's dress had rustled to the ground Jenna stepped back. Lisette had been wearing nothing underneath and was completely naked. Jenna saw her rival's body for the first time – but she was more than a rival, or about to be.

Pendulous, Nick had called Lisette's breasts on several occasions but that was unnecessarily cruel. Tentatively at first, Jenna cupped them in her hands; then, finding it was pleasurable, she caressed them more firmly. Sure, they were softer and lower than Jenna's own, but conical was a better word. After all, Lisette was more than ten years older. Her nipples were large, dark discs where Jenna's were snub-nosed, berry-like. She was fascinated by the contrast and bent her head to kiss each one in turn, tenderly. A throaty sound came from Lisette, half way between a chuckle of approval and a murmur of pleasure.

Abruptly she stepped back from Jenna.

'It was your idea to go skinny dipping,' she said. 'So what about it?'

She turned and ran splashing into the lake.

Jenna quickly rid herself of her briefs, stockings and suspenders. Then, as an afterthought, she unscrewed her antique-style earrings and placed them carefully on her jumble of clothes. She had pierced ears, but those earrings had come with the costume. She didn't want to risk losing them to the mud at the bottom of the lake.

Then she ran after Lisette. She gasped as the cold water hit her thighs but Lisette was already waist-deep, splashing her and calling her to come over.

In the middle of the lake, with the water gently lapping at their breasts, they kissed again. Jenna had never imagined this feeling – pressed against the naked softness of another woman's body. She was going to enjoy being initiated into the possibilities of bisexuality. It seemed so right that Nick's wife should be the one to do it.

She was content to let Lisette take control. As their

tongues rolled around one another, the older woman's hands wandered over her body. They parted the cleft of her ass and she felt the shock of cold water there. One hand snaked round and a finger probed her labia.

'Well,' Robin's voice surprised them from the bank. 'Someone else seems to have had similar ideas.'

The women looked up. Robin and Morgan were standing on the bank in front of the abandoned boathouse. From the grins on their faces they were obviously enjoying the sight. For once Robin's snake wasn't coiled about his arm; perhaps he'd left it enjoying Cleopatra's warm curves.

Jenna had been prepared to spring guiltily away but she was being held tight. Lisette simply looked up at the men and laughed.

'We might have been here first,' she called, 'but we don't claim exclusive rights. Come on. Join us!'

Morgan's grin widened and he began stripping off his highwayman's costume. First, the shirt: his dancer's torso was every bit as well-muscled and lithe as Jenna had imagined it would be. Under the water Lisette's finger continued to tease her labia and kept her unable to stop thinking about sex.

Robin appeared to have no plans to join them in the water. He leant against the boathouse, retrieved what Jenna took to be a joint from behind his ear and lit up.

Morgan unzipped his thigh-length boots and his black leather trousers. As he did so, Lisette's hand curled round Jenna's left breast and squeezed as if in excitement. Morgan was wearing a dark, shiny thong beneath his trousers. The v-shape of his well-toned stomach muscles led the eye irresistibly to what lay beneath.

When he'd undone the thong and tossed it on to the grass they could see a thick thatch of dark curls surmounting his cock. It was still soft for the moment but – the women's arms tightened about each other in mutual anticipation – they knew that very, very shortly it was going to be hard and one or other of them was going to feel it.

Morgan waded into the lake. He dived under the water and came up again behind the two women. Then he put an arm round each of them, cupping Lisette's breast in his right hand and Jenna's in his left.

If they'd been expecting a leading ballet choreographer to be refined then they were wrong.

'God, you two are like a feast for a starving man,' he said. 'D'you know how boring it is looking at female dancers all day? Flat chested, the lot of them – even if they would all fall into bed with me at the drop of a tutu. Now, two pairs of gorgeous big tits . . .' Here he paused for several moments and gave his full attention to fondling them appreciatively. 'If this water wasn't so cold I'd be in danger of coming right now. Which one of you fancies rubbing my cock?'

Jenna reached down in the water and tightened her right hand round his erection. She massaged it vigorously.

'Mmm,' Morgan sighed. 'That feels good. Oh, and I love the way your tits shake as you do it.'

'Perhaps we've all had enough cooling off,' Lisette murmured – with an edge to her voice, Jenna thought, as if resentful she wasn't getting her full measure of attention. 'We could continue this on dry land.'

Morgan nodded his agreement. He took each of them by the hand and together they splashed their way back to the dark, grassy bank. His cock was high and it trembled outrageously as he ran. Jenna looked at it unashamedly. It was long and perhaps a touch slimmer than Nick's but it had a very slight upward curve to it. She wondered how that would feel inside her.

But is it going to be me he fucks or her? she wondered. Lisette might have awoken new and unexpected desires in her, but Jenna still felt, even here, she was the competition.

Robin was leaning against the boathouse, taking slow, measured pulls at the long joint. Its exotic fragrance lingered on the still, humid air. That was part of the strange masculine scent that hung around him but not, Jenna realised, the whole of it.

Morgan turned to the two woman – graceful, in control, as if he were choreographing another dance.

'Lie down,' he whispered to Jenna, 'and spread your legs wide.'

So it is going to be me, she thought, and obeyed him without a word, trying to keep the triumph out of her eyes.

Morgan moved to stand behind Lisette and cupped her low, swinging breasts in his hands. He fondled them for a moment, apparently in no hurry. Lisette closed her eyes and tipped her head back against him in rapture. On the ground, Jenna twisted from side to side impatiently.

'Now,' Morgan said throatily in Lisette's ear, 'when we came along I believe you were on the point of initiating this tasty young woman into the rites of Sappho. So . . . as you were. Go down between her legs and tongue her out. Keep your ass high in the air for me, though.'

With the grace of a cat – and smiling her enigmatic smile again – Lisette did as she was told. Jenna began to panic. She'd been ready for Morgan's cock inside her. It might not happen.

But what Lisette's tongue was doing to her was exquisite. She seemed far more eager than Nick – and she could have taught her husband a few tricks! Her woman's tongue was more sensitive and mobile than a man's. And she was more aware of what another woman really craved. She flicked it back and forth between Jenna's labia, burrowed it into her like a warm, playful snake, then drew it out again and teasingly circled the knob of her clitoris. Jenna relaxed and surrendered to the inevitable. Initiation – that was the right word. She knew that after an orgasm from the Frenchwoman's skilful tongue, she would never be quite the same, sexually, again.

Jenna opened her eyes a crack. Morgan was still standing over them lovingly fondling his cock. He was getting off simply on the sight of two women's pleasure.

Lisette's tongue was keeping her hanging on the edge of gratification. Ripples of sensation were chasing each other around her vagina and up and over her mons. But she wouldn't come – she knew she wouldn't come. Not without her breasts being fondled first.

There was a reason for that. Ironically, Jenna had been one of the last girls in her class to 'develop'. From thirteen to sixteen she'd endured all the taunts. Then, magically, she'd blossomed into a generous double D. All the male attention previously reserved for other girls was now hers. And she'd loved it. The sweet novelty of having a big chest had never quite worn off. There was nothing guaranteed to turn her on more than having her lovers appreciate it too.

'Lisette,' she begged, 'Lisette – suck my tits. I can't come unless you do.'

Willingly Lisette prowled up along her body, leaving one fingertip resting on Jenna's tense clitoris. She took one of her peaked nipples in her mouth and fluttered her tongue around it. As before, she showed more finesse than her husband had ever done.

Morgan's grin widened. He appeared satisfied that some deeper, more intimate surrender had taken place. He knelt down and entered Lisette swiftly from behind.

Jenna felt the other woman's breathing quicken against her chest. Lisette, too, obviously took her greatest joy from a man's hard cock. She moaned loudly, intent now on the pleasure Morgan's thrusts were giving her. The pressure of her fingertip on Jenna's clit grew lazy.

But Jenna was very close to orgasm now. The kinkiness, the novelty of the whole situation sent her over the edge. Unrubbed though her clitoris was, a warm wave mounted slowly – all the more slowly for the easing off in stimulation – right through the centre of her body. Above her Lisette was shaking like a rag doll as Morgan's cock thrust as if he, too, couldn't wait a moment longer to come.

And the way Lisette was responding – Jenna began to wonder how much of the truth Nick had told her about his wife. Or even if he knew.

She must have dozed, she realised, after Morgan and Lisette – their animal need fulfilled – had rolled away from her, gasping. When Jenna opened her eyes both they and their clothes were gone. Robin was half lying beside her, propped up on one elbow. Even in the very dim light that reached across the water from the Hall, she could see the bulge his tense cock made in the front of his leather trousers.

He smiled as he caught her staring and seemed to read her thoughts. 'Not yet. Sometimes desire is a more powerful tool for being held back . . . You'll soon see.'

'Bloody voyeur,' she muttered. 'Do you get a kick out of watching other people do it?'

'You'd better believe it.'

Then he reached over to the pile of her discarded clothes and plucked the antique screw-on earrings from between the folds of cloth. He held one of them between forefinger and thumb for a moment and looked into the mellow depths of the stone, thoughtfully.

'Amber,' he said. 'Very Leo. Very masculine energy. Very special.' Then he paused a moment and smiled. 'Now I know how much you like your nipples being stimulated, here's a little something to be going on with.'

He reached over and screwed them, one at a time, on to the prominent tips of her nipples. She lay utterly passive and let him do it. The sensation was bizarre. Robin tightened the screw just to the point where he saw her wince with pain – and then, deliberately, just a little further. But the relentless pressure focused all her attention there. When the feeling of pain had passed – as her body got used to this extreme caress – she realised what this constant, low-level stimulation was doing to her.

Again, Robin seemed to be one step ahead. 'You'll

find someone to fuck you later on tonight,' he said. 'In fact, I'm sure you won't be able to help yourself by the time those little clips have had a chance to work. And believe me it'll be all the sweeter for having had to wait. Now, you'd better get dressed. I don't want to keep you from your party.'

Jenna scrambled to her feet and began pulling on her clothes. The dress was awkward with the zip at the back, but she was damned if she would ask Robin for help. He just stood there, watching her struggle, the line of his taut cock still disturbing the cut of his trousers.

Finally she managed it and laced up the front of her bodice. She was sure that the hard outlines of the earrings were visible through two layers of fabric.

'Have fun,' Robin called as she hurried across the rolling dark lawns. She didn't look back. 'I'll see you soon . . .'

She wondered how best to slip back into the party. Not through the French windows. Too obvious. Perhaps that side door, down the corridor and then back into the banqueting hall. People would just think she'd come back from the loo. Maybe.

But as she reached the hall Nick seized her wrist and dragged her back into the corridor. His face was flushed and he looked nothing like the carefree party host.

'You can start by telling me what the hell you've been playing at,' he snapped.

Chapter Three

STANDING IN THE corridor with Nick's hand like a vice around her wrist and the ends of her hair still damp from the lake, Jenna was acutely aware that she wasn't on the strongest possible ground. She took a deep breath and met her lover's eyes coolly.

'What do you mean?' she demanded.

'Running off and leaving Alex. I told you not to mess this up.'

Jenna let out the breath she'd been holding in a long sigh. So that was all he meant. The floodlights outside the Hall obviously didn't reach that far.

'Wasn't it you who told me,' she said with a smile, 'that the best bait is to leave someone wanting a little more? I'm not through with Alex yet.'

Nick's brutal grip on her arm relaxed and, in spite of himself, he smiled. 'Touché,' he said. 'You've always got an answer, haven't you?'

'I know. That's what you see in me.'

'So where the hell were you?'

'It's a hot, sticky night. Lisette and I fancied a swim in the lake.'

She watched, with satisfaction, the muscles at his

jaw twitch as he took this in. He was obviously picturing his wife and his lover naked together in the water. But was he picturing anything more? For the second time that evening Jenna wondered how well Nick understood Lisette.

He doesn't, she decided. He doesn't know. And I do. I've got something on him.

'Naughty schoolgirls, eh?' he murmured. 'I see I'm going to have to take at least one of you firmly in hand . . .'

With that he let go of her wrist completely and moved his hands to cup her breasts. He fondled them as if it had been torture to keep away from them for so long. Then the pads of his thumbs brushed her nipples.

'Jenna, what the hell. . . ?'

'My earrings,' she said tersely, 'are clamped to my nipples. No – don't ask. It's a long story.'

The muscle in his jaw twitched again. He wanted to ask, she knew that. But he wouldn't. It would be like admitting there was something he didn't know – or couldn't control.

'Oh, but Nick,' she continued quickly, 'the feeling of it . . . You know what I'm like. It's got me so horny I'm going crazy. Please, can't we just slip off and—'

Nick smiled. She was begging for it and he was back where he wanted to be.

'No,' he said firmly. 'Not now. You've cost me enough time with your antics. I've got to get back and circulate. But if you want to take them off I suggest you go into the conservatory. It'll be dark and quiet in there. If you're that desperate you could even lie back on the couch and let your fingers do the walking.' He grinned again. 'Knowing you, I'm sure it won't spoil your appetite for later.'

He turned and went back into the hall. The noise from the party burst on her for just a moment as the door swung open then closed. Jenna turned back down the corridor, away from the throng, towards the overstated Victorian conservatory that jutted out from the side of Netherdean Hall. Or was it more properly called an orangery when it was this big?

Nick was right: it was dark – and quiet. She sat down on a chaise longue and loosened the front of her bodice – again. She sighed with relief when it was all undone. It was one sort of pleasure having her breasts bound, thrust up and very aware of themselves, but it was another kind of pleasure to set them free.

She twisted an arm up behind her and undid the zip. She was, she thought wryly, getting good at this. She slipped her arms out of the sleeves and folded down the dress until she was naked from the waist up.

Jenna undid the earrings – a little reluctantly at the very last. It had been torture, yes, but of the sweetest kind.

Moonlight was falling on her through the mottled panes of old glass high above. In its light, the whiteness of her full breasts was more obvious than ever, and the shadows of her cleavage deeper. Jenna cupped her breasts proudly for a moment. Her fingers were tempted to stray across her aching nipples. She felt very, very inclined to follow Nick's parting suggestion.

'Well,' came the deep drawl from the shadows, 'that's a mighty inviting sight.'

Jenna froze, one hand still cupping her left breast. The voice had come from a period chair and the man it belonged to had been hidden in the shadows when she'd come in. He'd watched her undress and fondle herself. The voice had been American. As far as she was aware only one of those was on the guest list.

Alex rose from the darkness of the Regency chair. He'd taken off his cavalry officer's jacket but otherwise he was still in uniform. He came slowly round to stand in front of Jenna, enjoying her semi-nakedness in a way that, she suspected, had as much to do with 'getting one over on her' as the purely sexual.

'Didn't you make me look the fool?' he continued softly. 'There I was, wandering round with a drink in each hand, looking for all the world like a spare part. No one ever teach you manners this side of the Atlantic?'

Jenna opened her mouth, but couldn't think of anything to say. This was all getting hopelessly out of control. She was supposed to be playing Alex like a trout on a line – seducing his mind, reeling him in to become part of Nick's schemes. Instead she was sitting before him, bare-breasted, and words, her stock in trade, had deserted her.

'I'm here now,' she whispered eventually in a small, cracked voice.

'Damn right you are,' Alex replied and began to unbutton his flies.

This definitely wasn't supposed to be happening. Nick would be furious ... wouldn't he? He'd snapped his glass in anger when she'd teased him about whether or not she should take Alex to her bed. But – the thought kept nudging itself forward – had Nick known the American would be waiting in the dark conservatory? Had she been set up?

She was shaking with suppressed rage. But other instincts were surfacing, too, and anger merely put an unexpected edge on her frustrated desire. Her eyes were drawn to the front of Alex's trousers. She couldn't pull her gaze away. One by one, slowly as if he was deliberately teasing her, he undid his button fly. Then he reached in lovingly and withdrew his cock.

Earlier in the evening she'd suspected Alex had a well-toned body for a man his age. She could see the muscles at the base of his stomach – and yes, she'd been right, they looked tight. His cock was flaccid and, like many American men's, circumcised. Jenna was fascinated. She'd never seen a 'cut' one before. Unlike many women, she enjoyed the sight of a limp cock. She thought of it as a challenge.

Alex presented his naked glans to her lips.

'I wouldn't normally offer a young woman a pistol that didn't have any lead in it,' he murmured wryly, 'but this old soldier's seen a bit too much action already this afternoon. So suck it. Just enough to make me hard.'

She ran her tongue first along the underside of his cock. The stem began to swell and thicken with almost no hesitation. She flickered her tongue around the edges of his bulbous glans, curious and excited by the smoother contrast with all the intact men she'd known before. By this time his erection was pulsing and strong. She took Alex fully in her mouth.

At once he slipped his fingers into her wavy hair and pressed her close to his body. She felt herself almost smothered by his crisp pubic hair. She worked on him – her tongue flicking like a quick violinist's bow on the underside of his penis, her lips massaging up and down his shaft – until his erection had forced her jaws achingly far apart. Then Alex stepped back.

'Kneel up on the couch facing me,' he told her. Jenna obeyed.

'That's what I like to see,' he murmured slowly, 'a big, firm pair of tits in all their glory, bathed in the moonlight. Did you know you've been driving every man in this place crazy with them this evening – including me? Now I'm going to cream up all over them.'

He nestled his stiff cock in her cleavage and cupped her breasts, drawing them close together. His proud male organ was snug between them. He began to thrust up and down.

'You've got a fine pair for doing this,' he muttered. 'I bet I'm not the first guy, am I? My God . . . I'm going to come soon . . .'

He was right; she'd done this with Nick and other lovers besides. She loved the feeling of it. She loved the snaking shaft leaving its slick trail on her oh so sensitive skin. And Alex's hands, groping wildly at her, were giving her immense pleasure, too. If he'd thought using her body like this was some sort of payback humiliation, he was wrong.

Suddenly Alex gave a loud, low groan and, good as his word, climaxed abundantly over her throat and the upper curves of her breasts. He stepped back and looked for a moment at her glistening upper body, as if pleased with his work. Then he began to button his fly again.

'But . . . but . . .' Jenna began to protest.

'But you want to know what I'm going to do for

you in return? Absolutely nothing, little lady. As a lesson to you in not to be a prick tease.'

Then he was gone. But as the moonlight shifted round, she could see that he'd left his Confederate uniform jacket draped over the antique chair. She used it to wipe his spunk from her breasts, smiling perversely as she wondered how he'd explain that to his fancy-dress hire company. When she was fully dressed again she went back to the banqueting hall.

Nick wasn't there. It was late now and only a few knots of guests were left, none of whom Jenna knew. She became very aware she'd missed out on the buffet. A few slices of cream gateau were left at the far end of the table. She stuffed them all into her mouth in quick succession, not caring that she got cream all over her lips and fingers – not even when one or two worse-for-wear guests nudged each other and gave her sideways looks. Her immediate hunger satisfied she went off to find Nick – with one or two scores to settle.

Nick's room was half a landing away from hers. Planned that way, she suspected: near enough for easy access but not so close as to risk Lisette hearing them. In her present mood she flung open the door without knocking.

Nick, dressed only in a towelling robe, whipped round.

'You idiot,' he snapped when he realised it was Jenna. 'You could have blown everything. What if Lisette had been here? Oh, don't worry, she isn't. I don't know where she is.'

'I'd have said I was here to talk business. And, Nick, we do need to talk.'

'Talk, eh? Last time all you wanted to do was fuck. Not here – okay? Your room.'

He grasped her elbow and hurried her along the landing, glancing backwards over his shoulder several times towards the wide staircase but no one came.

'What's so urgent?' he said when her bedroom door was firmly closed behind them.

'Did you set me up with Alex, you bastard?'

'I don't know what you're talking about.'

'He was in the conservatory. Of course, I didn't realise that till I was naked from the waist up. Did you?'

Amusement twisted the corner of Nick's mouth. 'Of course not. You think I'd have sent you in there to strip off if I had? You know that's not how I play things, Jenna. So . . . he didn't fuck you, did he?'

'No. He rubbed himself off between my tits.'

Nick grinned, his anger apparently mellowing. 'I bet you enjoyed that. Seriously though, Jenna, you've let this get out of hand. This isn't like you. Steer clear of Alex for the rest of the weekend. Perhaps you were right. Perhaps I ought to get Lisette to handle him.' He pulled a slight face. She knew perfectly well his opinion of his wife's sex drive. 'I think I can trust *her* not to get out of control.'

It was Jenna's turn to smirk, then, and she hoped he didn't ask her why.

Out of control, she thought. Yes, we're all getting a little out of control. And the weekend's barely started.

'So,' Nick said, slumping into a wicker chair beside her dressing table, 'you still mad at me?'

'I'm not sure.'

'How "not sure"? "Not sure" enough to let me give you one?'

'You've fucked me often enough in the past when we've both been mad at each other and you know it.'

'Yeah, don't I just. And somehow I think those were the times you liked it best.'

Nick undid the belt of his towelling robe. He was wearing nothing underneath. His cock was resting on one thigh but he made no move to massage it into life. He folded his hands behind his head and looked up at her.

'You seem to have been taking your clothes off quite a bit this evening,' he said. 'Don't you think it's time you took them off for me? Just down to the stockings and suspenders, mind.'

She unlaced the bodice yet again. Then unzipped the dress, let it rustle to the floor and stepped out of it. Nick's cock was beginning to swell and darken against his thigh. She shimmied her shoulders, making her breasts jiggle in his face. Then she cupped them and rolled her own nipples between her thumb and forefinger, displaying herself for him. She knew what that did to Nick. By the time she slid her lacy briefs down over her stockinged thighs, his cock, even unrubbed, pointed straight up to his navel. She loved this bit. The evidence of her power over him.

He was right, though. She'd spent the last eighteen months infuriated with him for one reason or another – usually his arrogance and manipulation. But it was something that gave sex an extra edge.

'On the bed,' he told her. 'All fours. Make sure you can see yourself in the mirror and stick your ass in my face.'

She did, obediently. In the full-length mirror on the far wall she could see her breasts dangling down, gravity making them look bigger than ever. She saw

Nick get up, shrug his dressing gown from his shoulders and stand beside her.

He grabbed the twin hemispheres of her ass, framed by the black suspender straps, and moulded them in his hands for a moment. Though Nick was very overtly a breast man – and made no secret of it – sometimes for a change he enjoyed paying attention to her other full, white globes. And sometimes, when he was fondling them this brusquely, Jenna wondered what it would feel like to be spanked. She was wondering right now. She was on the point of asking him. But Nick . . . Despite the frequency of his appetite Nick was quite conventional about sex. Then it occurred to her that he wasn't the only man here this weekend.

Nick climbed on to the bed. He entered her swiftly from behind. Jenna let out a long sigh – and there was nothing calculated about it. All evening she'd longed for this simplest of sexual pleasures: to feel her aching, empty vagina filled by a man's good hard cock. Nick began to fuck her slowly.

They both looked ahead into the mirror. The view of their bodies turned them both on. Nick reached round to feel her breasts again. She enjoyed the sight of that. She enjoyed the slow, rhythmic thrusts of his cock so deep inside her. And then, almost as a peace offering, he reached round and gave her a rare gift.

It was almost unheard of for Nick to do anything to her sexually that wasn't primarily for his pleasure. But now he let go of one dangling breast and glided that hand down to toy with her pouting clitoris. His fingertip rubbed her bud in tiny circles, keeping time with his smooth cock thrusts.

Sexually she couldn't have asked for more. Breasts,

quim, clitoris – all receiving their full measure of attention. Nick could often be a selfish lover, but he was a skilled one when he chose to be. She surrendered to the delicious feelings that were playing tag all over her body. Her orgasm rippled up through her core, slow and fulfilling as it always was when both her clitoris and vagina were pleasured in perfect unison.

When Nick realised she'd come he turned his full attention back to her breasts and squeezed and rolled them until she felt his cock jerk and his climax burst into her.

He withdrew from her slowly and kissed both cheeks of her ass.

'I'd better go back,' he said, retrieving his robe, 'and see if my wife has put in an appearance. You do realise, don't you, I've not had a moment alone with her since she got back from Paris? I only hope she's not as horny as you tonight. If she wants me to get it up again she's going to have to do some pretty nifty mouthwork. And then she's going to wonder why . . .'

Lisette half stumbled as she ran across the rising lawns up to the Hall. She had to stifle a laugh. The evening had begun tediously. But it was getting sweeter and it wasn't over yet.

She smiled as she remembered Jenna – dear, innocent Jenna – squirming beneath her and begging for what would give her pleasure. And it had been all the sweeter that Morgan had chosen her – not her husband's nubile mistress – to receive his cock.

Oh yes, she knew about Nick and Jenna. And she wasn't the only one who knew. It struck her as almost

53

laughable that Nick thought she never suspected his affairs. How Anglo Saxon. She wasn't stupid. A photographer by training: the observer. She was much more adept at reading body language than he gave her credit for.

She stopped by a leaning yew, rested against it and caught her breath. She'd been running with a fire in her body. It was still raw from the eagerness of Morgan's cock.

They'd left Jenna half swooning by the lakeside and stolen off into the woods. There they'd stopped to explore each other's bodies again. Morgan had a dancer's unexpected strength. He'd lifted her off her feet as easily as if she'd been one of his fragile ballerinas and brought her down again, precisely, impaling her on his cock as if it was another, practised dance.

She'd taken her pleasure, then, from his body as he supported her weight and he'd held his own climax back. Then he'd bent her backwards over a fallen log and mounted her again. Sharp pieces of bark from the log had bitten into her skin and Morgan's athletic lovemaking had verged on brutal. She'd closed her eyes and surrendered to the delicious pleasure-pain of it. Still, when she'd whispered to him what she really wanted, even Morgan had demurred.

Lisette reached the Hall. Sex always gave her an appetite. She was starving. She knew by now she'd missed the main buffet but on the other hand she knew where the kitchens were. She let herself in.

She found some crusty bread. And a large bowl of guacamole in one of the fridges. She scooped up the guacamole with the bread and then, when the bread was finished but there was still plenty of dip to go, she scooped it up and licked it off her fingers. How she loved anything made with avocado: its texture, its silkiness, its sheer sensuality. She'd been disappointed to learn it was actually good for you.

The door clicked open and a wedge of light fell into the room.

'Thought I'd find you here,' the Texan voice mused. 'Hungry as ever?'

Lisette straightened up and smiled. 'I hope I'm not becoming predictable.'

'No, but by God your husband is. How did anyone as naïve as he is get to be such a big shot? You know he's been trying to sweeten me up with that well-endowed marketing girl of his?'

Lisette laughed. 'I'd guessed. Come here, Alex. Let's forget about business for once.'

'For once? You've got a short memory. I can think of a woman who called her husband on her mobile phone from a lay-by near High Wycombe and told him a string of lies about her flight being delayed and all the while her other hand was getting out my dick.'

'So, I've got a bad memory. Nick's always putting me down for it. Come here, Alex. Remind me.'

He closed the kitchen door and crossed the floor towards her. She put her hand down the front of his cavalry trousers.

'He's been busy,' she stated. 'Did you have our little Jenna after all?'

'Only as an appetiser. Not as a main course.'

Then he burrowed his hand up under her wide brocade Heroine of the Bastille skirts and ran two fingers between the moist lips of her quim.

'Well, if I'm not mistaken,' he said, 'you've been recently fucked as well.'

'A couple of appetisers. But definitely not main course. I know I can rely on you for that, Alex. Take off my dress.'

'Here?'

'Why not here?' She eyed the bowl of guacamole and then reached up to the rack above their heads and unhooked a fat, crinkled whole salami. 'We've got the necessary props.'

She turned her back on him and leant forwards a little over the work surface so he could undo her dress. He did and it slipped to the floor, leaving her totally naked beneath. Then he took a generous handful of the guacamole and creamed it into the cleft of her ass.

Lisette gasped involuntarily. The avocado dip was still cold from the fridge. But the coldness was bliss. She knew in a moment the fire would come.

Alex reached past her. The worktop was scattered with flaky crumbs of the bread she'd eaten greedily. He gathered some up and rubbed them into her low-hanging breasts. She murmured her appreciation as the sharpness of it bit into her skin.

'Ready?' Alex whispered.

'Ready, lover,' she replied and leant forwards a little further.

'Ready for what, Lisette?'

She smiled. He liked to hear her ask for it. 'My pussy's been rubbed raw by an amateur. I'm ready for you to slip in the back door instead.'

She heard him chuckle in a sort of triumph and he placed his cock head on the pursed ring of her anus.

Generously lubricated by the guacamole, Alex slipped in.

'Mmm,' he sighed. 'I don't know what it is about you French women that you like being buggered so much. But I'm sure glad you do.'

Lisette reached for the thick salami and slipped it as an impromptu dildo into her quim.

'You're going to eat this afterwards,' she told him. 'Then if you're really lucky I might let you lick the avocado out of my ass.'

She leant forwards again and let Alex bugger her with a delicacy yet a thoroughness few outside her native France could even begin to match. Certainly her very English husband would have been in for a shock. She sighed and pressed her breasts down against the cold metal counter. Extremes of sensation delighted her. There were still a few sharp crust-flakes left on the work surface and she ground these against her nipples. The pain and pleasure were so close.

She worked the salami in and out between her vaginal lips as Alex continued slowly to thrust his cock into her ass. The sheer dirtiness of it never wore off for her. The thought of its forbiddenness as much as anything tipped her over into a long, slow, rolling orgasm.

When Alex had climaxed too she made him kneel before her and eat the salami out of her quim. It protruded, fleshily, like a cock. It was as if he was going down on a man, performing the ultimate cannibalistic oral sex. Her head reeled with the outrageousness of it.

'Poor Nick,' she murmured afterwards. 'He really doesn't have the first idea.'

Alex looked at her strangely. 'I know he's your husband but you're not going all sentimental on me are you – not now?'

'Of course not. And besides ... I have a feeling Nick is going to end up thanking us.'

Chapter Four

JENNA STRETCHED AND rolled, alone on the wide bed, still not fully awake. One cotton sheet lay on her body like a whisper. She was wearing nothing underneath.

She arched her back and rubbed her shoulders against the firm mattress, feeling decidedly cat-like. She'd had the cream. Last night she'd had an unbelievable range of sexual experiences after which – particularly her unexpected pleasure from Lisette's mobile tongue – she didn't think she'd ever be the same again. And yet Nick's had been the only cock to enter her. She was still the faithful mistress – and the absolute whore.

From the angle of the morning sun she guessed it must be far later than her usual waking up time, even without groping for her watch. Who cared? She flung aside the sheet and let the sunlight fall directly on to her body. Her thighs rolled open and she welcomed a warm shaft of it between her legs. Its glow penetrated her, filling her body more completely, more deeply than any lover. She ran both hands over her breasts, taking a purely selfish pleasure in their weight and firmness. Desire was never far away.

Her bedside phone began to ring.

For a moment she wondered whether to ignore it, resenting the intrusion into what had been shaping up to be a particularly slow and sensual masturbation. But then a cloud moved across the sun; the warm shaft no longer nudged her quim. The mood was broken. She answered the phone.

'Hello, lazy,' came Nick's voice. 'I thought you were never going to pick it up. What were you doing?'

'Playing with my tits and thinking of you,' she murmured sleepily.

'I think we can go one better than that. Come to my room.'

'Where's Lisette?'

'She went horse-riding with Heather. They won't be back all morning. Come on. I've ordered us breakfast.'

'Give me ten minutes to have a shower.'

'Don't be too long. I've got a morning glory hard on and it's all yours if you hurry. Otherwise, it's driving me that crazy I might just have to toss myself off.'

I hope switchboard aren't monitoring these calls, she thought as she put the phone down. Still, in a place like this they ought to be used to such goings on . . .

Fifteen minutes later, showered and more awake, she wrapped a short, silk kimono round her still-damp body and padded down the corridor between her room and Nick's.

'Come in,' he called when she knocked on the door. 'I left it open.'

Jenna made a point of locking it behind her. 'Suppose it hadn't been me? Suppose it had been a chambermaid instead?'

'If she'd been a nice, slightly plump nineteen-year-old with a short black skirt and rather well endowed and wobbly in the chest department, then she'd have got what's waiting for you instead.'

Nick loved to do that: teasing her to try to make her jealous. And the infuriating thing was it worked. He knew it. It kept him in control.

He was lying naked on the bed, propped up on one side. His cock was very, very erect, the skin shiny under the strain of how much blood was pumping through his proud male organ. Beside him on the bed was a tray of fresh fruit, much of it exotic. He was grinning.

'Get 'em off and lie down here,' he said. 'We're having breakfast off each other.'

Jenna undid the belt on her kimono and let it slide off her, right there by the door. Then she sashayed slowly across the room, enjoying the way Nick's gaze was riveted to her. He might like his power games, but she could play them too. Even after eighteen months she knew damn well he couldn't get enough of her firm, curvy body. And that was the sort of attention she loved.

She lay down beside him on the bed, her curiosity pleasantly piqued as to what was going to happen next.

Nick took two hulled strawberries from a piled-high bowl and placed them carefully over her nipples. Their prominent tips fitted snugly into the holes in the fruit. For a moment he left them there, admiring. And she looked down her body and saw the red teats, outrageously large and erect. Then, slowly, first one then the other, Nick ate them off her breasts.

He kept on replenishing them, eager and fascinated by the symbolic mummy-baby devouring of her body. After a while the juice from the strawberries began spilling down between her breasts, gathering in rivulets in her deep cleavage. Nick lapped the juice enthusiastically. Jenna shivered in response. How she loved her breasts being pleasured.

When the bowl was half empty, Nick stopped abruptly. 'Your turn. Choose a piece of fruit and do what you like with it.'

She picked up half a ripe, stoned mango and rubbed it into his cock. Nick moaned his appreciation. The fruit had soon disintegrated into pulp, smothering his straining erection. Jenna wriggled down the bed and ran her tongue up and down his organ, licking up every last trace of the mango flesh.

Nick groaned in frustration. 'If you sucked me now I think I'd explode.'

'No chance,' she countered. 'You started this game. Your turn again. No – I'm going to choose the fruit. And where it goes.'

She peeled a thick banana. Obvious it might have been, but she knew she was going to enjoy this. She pushed the fruit as high into her quim as it would go and then she lay back on the bed, her thighs spread wide.

'Eat it,' she commanded – and Nick did.

Jenna writhed under the pleasure of his tongue – all the more so because she knew cunnilingus wasn't something Nick did willingly. Still, she thought wryly, his wife did a better job if only he knew it. But the way his jaws worked as he ate and sucked the banana from her gave the occasion an extra frisson. It was sweet, sweet torture but it left her hanging just short of the brink of orgasm. Finally she surrendered to her overriding need.

'Okay, okay,' she gasped. 'Game's over. I want your cock inside me.'

Nick raised his face from her bush.

'No chance,' he echoed her deliberately with a grin. 'If I stuck my horny cock in your tight little pussy right now, how long d'you think I'd last? About ten seconds, max, and that wouldn't be much good to you. No, you're going to suck me, Jenna. Suck my cock. It's ages since you have. And if you don't I might just have to go and remind myself how well Eleni does it . . .'

It wasn't jealousy that made her do it – no, she refused to admit that it was jealousy. But Nick really did have such a suckable cock. She scrambled down the bed, swapped places with him and engulfed his taut erection with her mouth.

As always, it forced her jaws wide apart. She could feel the swollen veins pulsing against her lips as they pumped him up to bursting point. She flicked her tongue along the underside of his organ and then around and around the tip. Almost at once he came, copiously, and Jenna swallowed it all.

Nick withdrew from her mouth and they shifted on the bed till they were level with each other.

'You can always get me stiff again,' he said. 'You know how to do it.'

It was true, she did. And though she knew part of Nick was all the more addicted to her for it, she knew part of him resented her for it too.

Nick got turned on by someone playing with his

nipples. Jenna had discovered that early on, almost by accident, as she'd brushed against them once in foreplay. He almost hated her knowing it – hated the fact that he responded like a woman when as far as he was concerned everything should be centred around his aggressively male cock.

But respond he did. She smiled as she remembered the times she'd lain on top of him, kept his flagging cock in place with her tight vaginal muscles and sucked his broad, flat nipples, making him stiffen inside her so they could fuck a second time.

She began to run her fingers through the hair on his chest but he grasped her arm and pinned it back against the mattress.

'Not yet,' he said. 'I think those juicy tits need a bit more of a seeing to first.'

When he did this she felt so exposed – so deliciously exposed. She strained against him because she knew it turned him on to see her struggle. Nick, though he was psychologically good at controlling people, had never played physical domination games with her.

She wouldn't have objected. In fact, once or twice, she'd been on the point of asking Nick to tie her wrists and ankles to the bed – to spread her legs so wide she was stretched and helpless and unable to concentrate on anything but his powerful thrusts as he had sex with her. But she'd held back. Nick might be shocked. Here, though, in this house, on this weekend, maybe she'd get the chance. She had the feeling anything could happen.

Nick freed her arm and reached for the strawberry bowl again. He placed two more ripe strawberries over the tips of her nipples and ate them off slowly and with obvious enjoyment. When they were gone he kept reaching for more and more. Jenna lay back, yielded, and her head was filled with the fantasy that he was devouring her flesh.

'That's started me going again,' he murmured when the fruit bowl was empty. 'Your turn. Do it.'

He lay back on the bed this time and Jenna rolled on top of him. She bent her head and, keeping the muscular tip of her tongue as firm as she could, drew tiny circles with it on Nick's flat, dark nipples. He closed his eyes and moaned. The sound was almost as urgent as if she'd been sucking his cock. If her lips and tongue hadn't been so busy she'd have grinned in triumph. Nick didn't always have the upper hand. She enjoyed times like these.

Against her belly she could feel that Nick's cock had fully hardened. But she kept tormenting his nipples until his moaning took on a different note and he begged her to stop.

'Enough,' he whispered. 'Ride me, Jenna. And let your tits hang down in my face.'

That was just what she wanted to do. She mounted his body, welcoming his stiff cock into her moist quim. It had been buzzing for this all morning. Slowly, slowly she lowered herself on to him, savouring the feeling as his firm erection filled her deeply. She played with the angle and tilt of her hips, trying out all the different ways of making his cock head stroke just the right spot inside her. Jenna rocked her pelvis slowly. Her own pleasure was the only thing that mattered to her now. If Nick came too that was almost incidental.

She leant forwards and dangled her breasts just out of reach of the mouth that gaped for them like a baby's. She made him crane his neck and strain to take one nipple in his mouth. She loved the stimulation of his lips and tongue, but she loved making him work for it too. It wasn't often she had Nick in this sort of position – physically or psychologically.

Insistently she ground her pubis against his until the tension built up and spasmed deliciously into her body. She was glad of Nick's firm cock; it stretched her vaginal muscles even as they relaxed and contracted involuntarily around it. And – although for an instant she considered leaving him there just to see what he would do if angry and frustrated – she carried on riding his body with piston-like fervour because truly she loved the feeling when a man's cock swelled inside her as he came.

Afterwards, as she lay down beside him on the bed, she realised from the way the sun had shifted from the window that it must be almost midmorning. Hours had passed.

'We don't often get to do this,' she giggled.

'What, fuck? We do that all the time, Jenna, what with you being such a horny little bitch.'

'No, I mean we don't often get to relax like this in a big double bed afterwards. It's strange, that's all.'

'Don't get used to it. You've always known we can't have that sort of affair.'

'You like everyone to think you're hard as nails, don't you, Nick? Goes with the image. Doesn't wash with me. I've seen your Achilles heel.'

'What do you mean?'

'Your sister, Heather. You're so protective of her. Even to the extent of using this party to try and put her in the way of a top London choreographer; it's as if you don't trust her to manage her own career. Well, it's just a shame that—'

'Heather's the only family I've got,' he snapped.

'And okay, if you must know, that's important to me. Oh, there's that brattish cousin on my dad's side – lost in some run-down hippy commune somewhere. But I've better things to do than chase after that bastard's side of the family.'

Jenna paused and chose her next words carefully. She'd never heard him speak about his father like that before. In fact she couldn't remember him speaking about his real father at all.

'You kept his surname, though,' she commented, 'even when you could have taken a new one when your mother remarried. And you changed the name of Lisette's company so it had your name stamped all over it – and your father's name come to that. How come, if you resent him so much?'

'Yeah – and you know why I did that? He was a fucking hippy, that's why. Commerce and capitalism were dirty words to him. So now every time I turn a profit and that profit's got "Treganza" written on it, it's like sticking two fingers up to him.'

'Wow, I was right about what I said last night. Freud would be sorry he never got to meet you.'

Nick glared at her darkly. 'Listen, when you're in my office, you're there to make sure the world knows how successful Treganza Leisure International is. And when you're in my bed it's because I like to shove my face between those well-developed tits and stick my cock into your tight, horny pussy. In neither case is it your job to get under my skin.'

Automatically she glanced down between his thighs. Nick had a semi hard on again. She'd noticed this before: like many male animals Nick began to get an erection instinctively as a display of aggression when threatened or angry.

'Well,' she murmured. 'I didn't realise I'd touched such a nerve. And did you have any plans for that...?'

He smiled coldly, as if pleased by the chance to hold something back from her. 'Not what you're thinking. But tonight – if you're a good girl. I've got the sort of entertainment planned – a treasure hunt – that'll mean we can slip off somewhere. But you'd better get dressed and make yourself scarce now. I can't imagine Lisette being that much longer.'

Heather's young body swayed automatically in time with the movement of her horse. It was, she'd decided quite early in the ride, almost like dancing. You had to let go of your preconceptions, lose your natural stiffness, allow your body to go with the flow. She was beginning to think she was getting quite good at it now – although, admittedly, they hadn't gone faster than a walking pace. Good enough, certainly, to relax and look around her. And take in what was going on.

Lisette and that American were riding directly in front of her, their stirrups almost touching as they manoeuvred to stay level on the narrow bridleway. There was something about their easiness together that Heather didn't like. Lisette was married to Nick. And for as long as she could remember, Heather's brother had been the biggest, most important thing in her life.

'It's just business, *chèrie*,' Lisette had whispered to her in that French accent Heather sometimes thought she exaggerated for effect. 'Don't worry. Nick has asked me to – how you say – butter him up.'

She'd lingered over the word 'butter' and a mischievous light had flicked on in her eyes. Heather had felt – as she frequently did with Nick's crowd – that someone had made an in-joke she didn't quite understand.

Some trailing honeysuckle caught her across the face and dragged her fair hair from its ponytail. When she'd recovered, Lisette and Alex were laughing again. Heather felt well and truly out of it. Ahead of them on the trail was the man who'd introduced himself as Robin and offered to be their guide for pony trekking out of the Hall grounds and into the wider, wilder woods beyond.

Stupid – why did I get myself stuck at the back? Heather wondered. Now, if I'd managed to get myself alongside him before the path got so narrow, this ride could have been much more interesting.

After only a few minutes more, though, the path splayed out as it met a brook. Heather took a deep breath and urged her pony into a trot, hoping to overtake Lisette and Alex before the trees closed in again.

Abruptly Robin reined in his mount. 'Let your horses have a bit of a rest and a drink here,' he said. 'It's a hot morning for them, too.'

The four horses drank slowly from the brook then cropped the grass patiently while their riders sat on the grass in the shade. The animals were clearly used to this routine. They didn't try to wander away.

Alex and Lisette continued to chat – inanely, Heather thought. She studied the more silent, pensive Robin as much as she could without seeming too obvious. She liked his dark hair and the way it gleamed as the dapples of sunlight fell on it. She liked the way it spilled in a liquid ponytail down over one shoulder.

Nick's business crowd were, on the whole, too

conventional looking for her tastes, even in their fancy dress. Last night she'd scanned the hall, looking for someone who'd make this trip away from college and London worth her while. There was some hidden agenda to this 'birthday bash', she was sure, but she couldn't work out what it was. Only Robin had seemed a serious possibility.

Of course, there was Morgan Heselton. Nick had all but admitted he'd included him on the guest list so that he and Heather could be introduced. But his reputation overawed her. She couldn't just go up to him and make herself known. Besides, he hadn't looked twice in her direction all evening. No, it was Robin who intrigued her. She'd never been out with a man who had a beard – a close-clipped, springy beard. She wondered what it would be like to touch.

Robin got to his feet and Heather was afraid he'd caught her staring. But he went over to the horses and seemed to be checking them over. He stayed with her grey pony the longest.

Eventually he straightened up and walked back to the others. 'Bad news, I'm afraid, Heather. Your pony's sprained something. Look how he's holding his front foot up – they only do that when something's very wrong. I can't risk you riding him back to the Hall and putting more strain on it. I'll lead him back – I know a short cut.'

'I'll come with you. I'll walk, I don't mind.'

'No, that's okay. You carry on and enjoy yourselves. To be honest the horses probably know this route by heart. Perhaps you could double up with Alex. His is a good strong horse and besides,' Robin grinned, 'you dancers never weigh a thing. That okay by you, Alex?'

'Sure,' the American drawled, then turned and smiled at Heather: the first time that morning he'd even appeared to notice she was there.

'Good man,' Robin said and clapped Alex on the shoulder.

That's when Heather noticed the scent. She thought she'd caught a whiff of it the previous night. It was musky, leafy and there was something entrancing about it, that momentarily seemed to dim the other senses.

When she looked up again Robin had mounted his chestnut mare and was riding back along the path. Lisette was on her horse and Alex was standing beside her holding his mount's reins.

'Well,' he said to Heather, 'how about it? You want to go in front or behind?'

'Er, I don't know. Behind, I guess.'

She swung up behind Alex and held him awkwardly around the waist. Fate had messed things up for her again. Why hadn't Robin volunteered to let her share his horse? He was far more her type. More her age – well, the gap was perhaps ten years rather than over twenty. If this had been Robin in front of her now, how much her hands would have enjoyed leaving his waist, roving down over and between his firm, leather-clad thighs ... That exotic scent she'd noticed in the clearing was still travelling with them.

Heather craned her neck to see over Alex's shoulder. Lisette was still in front. But her horse, encumbered by only one rider, was pulling away from them and disappearing further and further down the path.

She was very aware of the heat, despite the dappled shade of the sycamores above them. She was aware of the way the sweat was trickling between her small, firm breasts as they were crushed against Alex's moist back. And then she realised that her right hand had been making little circular motions on his chest as her fingertips explored the texture of his hair beneath his light T-shirt. Abruptly she stopped.

'You can carry on,' Alex murmured. 'That's nice. Almost adequate compensation for giving you a ride, little girl. If you wanted to do the same with your other hand, now that would be even better.'

Her left hand was resting by his denim-clad crotch. She wondered how it had got there.

'I'm sorry,' she gasped. 'I didn't . . .'

'No need to apologise.'

She felt the slight tension in his arms. The horse wasn't just falling behind under her extra weight. Alex was applying a subtle but definite pressure on the reins.

She was here to have fun. Isn't that what she'd heard countless other guests whisper to each other since the previous afternoon? And she knew damn well what they meant. She wasn't a virgin and she wasn't nearly as innocent as big brother Nick liked to think. Alex was older. He knew things. He could, after all, be a rich source of possibilities.

She untucked his T-shirt and began to run her fingers over his stomach muscles. They were firm. Good. With just a little scattering of crinkly hair. Alex murmured his approval and, encouraged, she crushed her breasts more tightly against his shoulder blades. Lisette's horse turned a corner away up the track and disappeared from sight.

'Your hard little tits feel good against my back,' Alex whispered. 'So good. But they're playing hell with my trapped dick. Do him a favour, Heather. Set him free.'

She felt her way down, unpopped the button on his jeans and unzipped his flies. Her fingers found the pulsing warmth of his cock and closed around it. From where she was she couldn't see it but she could feel it swelling and hardening in her hand.

Alex reined in with a grunt. 'I think we've gone as far as we can on horseback. Come on.'

He swung his leg over the horse's withers, cowboy fashion, and dismounted. He took off his Western-style hat and hung it on a branch. His scalp was bare and gleamed in the heat. Heather found his baldness off-putting and fascinating all at once. Alex held up his hands to help her down. But for the moment all she could do was stare at his cock.

She'd had several lovers at the dance school. But not enough that she was blasé about the first sight of a brand new hard on. Alex's was high, rising from between the panels of his jeans and poking straight at her. And his cock was circumcised. She'd never thought about whether she'd like that or not. But the aggressive, ever-ready display of his glans looked as if it would be constantly horny. A shiver went through her as she wondered what he was planning to do with it.

'Come on,' Alex repeated in his Texan drawl that could be at once both melodic and menacing. 'I didn't take you for a prick tease – Jesus, are all English women like you? You've started me off. Now what are you going to do about it?'

She held out her hands to him. He jumped her down. The horse wandered off just a few paces and patiently cropped the grass as if all this was really nothing new.

Alex grasped her shoulders and pressed her against a nearby tree, kissing her deeply, peremptorily. All the while his iron-hard cock jousted blindly against her crotch. The knobbly bark of the tree was biting into the backs of her bare thighs. But she found she rather liked the texture. She wondered how it would feel when the even softer skin of her bare ass was pressed against it.

'Undress me,' she whispered but Alex was already tugging at the buttons on her skimpy shorts.

There was something about the way he'd never asked permission. With her other lovers, every move had been prefaced by, 'Can I. . . ? Do you mind. . . ?' But Alex was beyond that. She rolled the words round in her head: 'Taken', 'Ravished by an older man'. She found they turned her on.

Alex pulled her T-shirt off and flung it to the ground. Then he slipped off the stiff lace bra that gave her small breasts extra uplift. There was none of the awkward fumbling she was used to. When she was completely naked he ripped off his own T-shirt and pressed his body again on hers, grinding the crisp hairs on his torso into her sensitive young breasts.

'So tell me, my little English rose,' he murmured, 'I often find you girls are full of surprises. Just how would you like to be fucked?'

'You decide,' she whispered submissively.

'Do I get the impression you'd like to be dominated? Hmm . . . Better and better. Let's see what we can do.'

He whipped out the leather belt from around his jeans. He still hadn't fully taken them off and they were hanging round the tops of his thighs, framing his cock and implying an urgency of desire that dispensed with the need to get properly undressed.

Before she'd realised what he was doing he'd backed her right up to the tree and pinned her wrists behind it, leaving her breasts thrust out, inviting and very, very vulnerable. Then he lashed her wrists together behind the tree with his leather belt. He could do what he wanted to her now. She was helpless.

Alex bent his head, devouring first one thrust-out breast then the other. He seemed to be able to get virtually the whole of each in his mouth. His bare scalp was so close to her now. She'd have liked to touch it, to see what sensual possibilities might be there. Her fingertips tingled with curiosity. But she was bound.

His tongue snaked and flickered around her nipples mercilessly. Heather writhed in this almost overkill of pleasure but she could hardly move. He'd tied her body so tightly. She eased her thighs apart, ready to receive his upstanding cock.

He took the hint and thrust into her with one unhesitating movement – so fast and sure it took her by surprise. He grasped a tight breast in each hand and, as he fucked, fondled them brusquely, as if he had an absolute right to them which, as far as Heather was concerned, for that hour in the forest, he did.

He was driving into her like the steam-driven shaft of a precision machine. Any of Heather's younger lovers would have climaxed by now and that would have been that. But Alex knew what he was doing. His thrusts were pressing her tender buttocks into the bark, making them tingle, making her aware of their erogenous possibilities for the very first time.

His bony pubis squeezed her pulsing clitoris every time his shaft hit home. He was riding her body furiously and she knew later she'd be sore, but for now she just enjoyed it as her climax rose from her mons Veneris and shivered deep into her tight young quim.

'You almost-virgins are so good to fuck,' he whispered. 'So tight. Nearly as sweet as buggering a well-clenched ass.'

Heather drew a breath in sharply at the thought. But what shocked her seemed to arouse Alex even more. He began thrusting faster. But he still didn't seem to be on the verge of coming. His cock was as forceful as ever and he seemed to know exactly what he was doing. As the warm waves of her first orgasm died away, to her amazement a second mounted in her, even stronger and more muscular than the first. Still Alex kept fucking her with absolute mastery. As the glow of her second orgasm melted away, Heather opened her eyes a crack. She thought she saw – or was it her imagination? – the flash of two horses, a chestnut and a grey, moving through the trees.

Chapter Five

BY MIDDAY JENNA was back in her own room. She couldn't settle. She felt hot and uneasy so she got dressed and went down to the lawns for a swim in the lake. But too many people were gathered on the banks and she didn't know any of them. She wasn't in the mood for repeating her skinny-dipping exploits. It was one thing at night, with the mysterious, cloaking semi-darkness wrapped around her; quite another in broad daylight in front of strangers.

In contrast to her waking mood that morning, she began to wonder why the hell she'd agreed to come. She was friends with virtually no one here – unless you could count Nick, which was questionable. She was supposed to have been working on that American over the investment deal and she'd even messed that up. The lawns were dotted with small groups of people enjoying each other's company – eating, drinking cool drinks, laughing. Jenna felt shut out of the party mood.

After negotiating half a circuit of the lake, she realised the tight, angry knot in her stomach was at least partly hunger. She went back to the Hall, followed trails of people heading for yet another buffet and helped herself to a pile of sandwiches, vol-au-vents and small spicy things that were probably some variation on meatballs. She ate at a table placed out of the way and kept her eyes on her food in case anyone tried to be friendly – she wasn't up to it. The food helped jolt her out of her mood. Whatever else, the catering couldn't be faulted: the creaminess of the vol-au-vents, the flakiness of the pastry, the sharp, aromatic contrast of the little cutlets.

She felt better, but still not particularly gregarious, and decided to go for a walk.

Jenna headed for the woods. They covered many acres of the hotel grounds but paths and bridleways linked to the greater part of the forest beyond. She could lose herself here for the rest of the afternoon.

As soon as she was deep beneath the trees her mood lifted. A cool breeze rustled the leaves, toying with the ends of her loose hair and making her curls caress the bare skin between her throat and the low neckline of her light print dress.

The woods were beginning to seduce her. The only sounds were birdsong and the rustle of the leaves. She touched the newly opened, slightly pink leaves on the nearest oak. They often put out new ones at this time of year. Lammas flush, she knew it was called, but where had she heard that? Lammas was the old name for August the first. Tomorrow.

She believed she was truly alone. She could do anything. The tendrils of air that curled around the exposed parts of her skin seemed more acutely physical. They were persuasive. They convinced her that if it was pleasant to feel them on her arms and throat, it would be so much more sensual on the softer, more intimate parts of her body.

As she walked Jenna undid the buttons, one by one, all the way down the front of her short, flimsy dress. When it was hanging open she let it fall to the path and didn't bother to pick it up. She hadn't been wearing a bra underneath, only briefs, and her breasts revelled in being exposed to the daylight and the cooling woodland air. Despite her adventures in bedrooms, hotel rooms or wherever else over the past few years, she'd rarely had the chance to take off her clothes in natural surroundings in the middle of the day.

Little wisps of her hair tumbled down her cleavage and flicked across the upper slopes of her breasts. Her skin welcomed this caress, more slowly sensual than any impatient lover's, more diffuse. It didn't occur to her to wonder how she'd explain this if she met another person. The forest seemed empty of all human sounds. She was alone.

After walking a few more minutes Jenna tugged at the tie-sides of her panties, first with her right hand, then with her left. She didn't even alter the rhythm of her walking and they slipped from between her legs and rested on the path. She was naked apart from her thonged leather sandals.

The breeze combed its fingers through her pubic hair. The cool air washed over the soft skin on her buttocks and crept into the moist cleft between. Any traces of frustration or resentment were long forgotten. There was something so liberating about being this exposed.

She really hadn't been paying attention to where she was going. She might, for all she knew, have still been in the hotel grounds, might have left them completely or might have crossed the path in and out of them a dozen times. Then she found the clearing.

It was a large clearing, roughly circular. Around the far edge a group of medieval-type tents had been erected. Jenna took a sharp breath when she saw them but the only movement was the flapping of one or two bright panels of canvas in the breeze. They seemed completely deserted. In the middle of the clearing last year's leaf litter had been carefully raked aside. And on the bare ground was a painted image.

Jenna took several paces further into the clearing to get a better look. At first sight it had reminded her of the Cerne Abbas giant, but this was more intricate, more detailed, more beautiful. It was also very clearly male. It had an enormous, erect phallus, out of all proportion to its height of roughly twelve feet. And in place of a man's head it had a lion's. Or perhaps it was supposed to be a mask, she wasn't sure.

The image made her feel strange. It was something that demanded her reverence – a work of art – and yet she felt compelled to offer herself to it sexually, too. The second compulsion became stronger. Jenna slipped out of her thonged sandals and prostrated herself on the lion giant.

At once she felt a strange sensation – almost, but not quite, physical – as if the giant's outrageously huge phallus had actually penetrated her. It was burning her, filling her, stretching her sex. It was taking root. She was too small to contain its huge dimensions. It was swelling inside her, threatening to burst her, paying her back for every time she might have wished for a lover with a bigger cock.

Abruptly her concentration was broken. There was a soft scuffle in the leaf litter behind her. Jenna rolled on to her back. Robin was standing over her.

She was naked beneath him, spreadeagled and vulnerable. Robin infuriated her. He had teased, frustrated and – she strongly suspected – manipulated her the previous night. But he was different. And she wanted him.

Perhaps this time, she thought. I am here. We are alone. I'm more than ready to be taken. Perhaps this time I'll see the cock which distorts those leather trousers so maddeningly.

The breeze had grown stronger. There was a slight shift in the leafy canopy high above. The mottled light fell on Robin at a slightly different angle.

That was when she noticed the snake. It had been still across his shoulders, camouflaged by the light and the dark. Now it began to travel, coiling itself sinuously round his right arm. When its head reached his hand, Robin bent down and laid it on her naked flesh.

Jenna tensed. The snake lay absolutely still again, its sinewy length sprawled over her belly, its tiny alert head between her breasts. She forced every muscle in her body to relax in turn. The snake was warmer than she'd expected. And the sensation of its weight on her body was not at all unpleasant.

'Relax,' Robin said at last. 'Lilith isn't dangerous – d'you think I'd carry her around with me if she was? She's not poisonous. A boa constrictor's not big enough to crush a human even if she wanted to. Which she doesn't, of course.

'And what was it you said to Nick last night? About Freud and snakes? You were right. Snakes are an ancient symbol of phallus worship. Relax and enjoy.'

Damn him, she thought. He's got ears everywhere.

How did he know what Nick and I were saying in a private conversation? And just what is he up to anyway?

But then the snake began to move. Its head nudged up between her breasts. She couldn't help but think of the pleasure Alex's cock had given her there the previous night. But this went on and on. Its length thickened as it glided up her cleavage then very slowly wrapped itself around her breasts in a figure of eight. It tightened ever so slightly, pulling her breasts together and offering them up for Robin to see. Thoughts of phallus worship filled her head.

Robin smiled as if well pleased by the sight of her entwined with the snake. Then he unzipped his leather trousers and took out his cock.

Jenna gasped, and his smile widened as if he delighted in her surprise. Robin's glans was pierced with a thick silver ring.

'Can you feel the giant beneath you?' he murmured. 'Can you feel your horniness seeping into him, making him come to life?'

She'd already felt it when she'd been alone with the image and lying face down upon it. Now she felt something stirring again, some energy. Every part of her body in contact with the cool, moist ground began to tingle.

'Feel his great cock rise beneath you,' Robin continued as, lovingly, he began to masturbate his own. 'Feel it rise and thrust itself into your juicy, willing sex.'

She did. She felt the burning sensation stretching her quim again as if the hugest cock imaginable was fucking her like a steam piston that would never tire, never come, never stop. Her whole body was pulsing.

The snake seemed to throb against her skin as it squeezed tighter round her breasts, making them stand high and proud with her nipples peaking in the cooler air.

For once she hadn't closed her eyes. Her attention was fixed on Robin's cock. He was standing over her like a tower, his shaft a great swollen stem that seemed to block out everything else. He was wanking furiously. She was sure it wouldn't be long before he let his semen spurt all over her belly and snake-bound breasts.

'Or maybe,' Robin continued breathlessly, 'you like being buggered. Perhaps you'd rather the giant's cock slipped up your dark, secret ass.'

As soon as he'd said it, it was happening to her. Her vagina and her asshole burned together with the presence of the tireless phantom cock. Anal penetration was something she'd never yet dared, although she'd fantasised about it often enough. The last forbidden hole. Now it was being satisfied with a hot brutality.

It flashed through her head that she'd read somewhere that some species of snakes had two penises. Her imagination conjured up a snake god. One who could penetrate his female followers anally and vaginally at the same time – could satisfy them utterly. The power of the image made her come.

It was a strange, prolonged sort of orgasm. It took her over, clasping the muscles of her anus and vagina but holding them there, balanced on the edge, a sexual freeze-frame that wouldn't let her go. Only when Robin's cock began to shoot its pent-up load wetly across her body did the wave release itself more deeply into her.

She'd never known a man climax so abundantly. He seemed to be coming and coming for ever, directing his sperm freely over her belly and breasts. It was as if the orgasm he'd denied himself by the lake the previous evening – and who knew how many others – were all happening at once. When at last he'd finished and his erection was beginning to fade, the snake unwound itself from her breasts and slithered off through the leaf litter towards one of the tents.

Jenna sat up and, without quite knowing what motivated her, she kissed the very tip of Robin's pierced cock.

'Don't ask,' he chuckled.

'What?'

'The "Did it hurt?" question. Everyone does. It's such a cliché. "Hurt" isn't the point. It was ... extreme. I approve of extremes.'

He zipped up his flies again, sat down beside her on the leaf litter and then, quite tenderly, began to massage his come into her breasts.

'Good for the skin,' he murmured. 'Helps maintain youthful elasticity. And let's face it, Jenna, a big girl like you needs to look after that skin. It's got quite a job to do. I think you ought to have blokes come all over your breasts as often as possible.'

'Don't worry. I do.'

She tipped back her head and simply enjoyed the feeling of his busy hands rubbing his come into her bobbing chest. Was she still infuriated by him? She couldn't quite decide. The feeling was strangely sensual rather than sexy. For once she wasn't getting aroused again.

'There,' Robin said and she realised he'd finished; his come was well and truly rubbed into her skin.

Like an animal, he had marked her with his scent. 'Now, just a little something to finish off . . .'

He reached, with difficulty, into the front pocket of his tight leather trousers and retrieved a small glass phial. He tipped something on to his forefinger and anointed her lower belly and breasts.

'That scent!' she exclaimed. 'What the hell is it?'

'Just some aromatherapy oils I blended specially for this weekend. Ylang ylang, mainly – and a few other things besides. Very warm and sensuous, don't you think? Very Leo.'

'I imagine it's already been responsible for a fair few indiscretions.'

'No. I mean, no it hasn't been responsible. It only helps take the edge off inhibitions and gives your real desires a chance to show through. It can't make you do anything you don't want to. And you'd be quite surprised what some people here want to do.'

'Actually I don't think I would. Leo,' she murmured, touching the outline of the image beneath them tentatively as if she was still in awe of its power. 'Is that what all this is about?'

'Mainly, yes. The king of the beasts. The wild masculine. Concentrating all sexual energy in one place. It's barely even started to come into play yet. Wait till tonight.'

'And the tents?'

'I put those up for outdoor entertainments.'

'Nick said we're having a treasure hunt tonight.'

'Did he now? Well Nick hired me to take care of the fun and games this weekend. Or, to be more accurate, he instructed someone who sent a memo to someone else who hired me. So things might not turn out quite the way he planned them. Speaking of which . . .' He glanced at his watch. 'I expect you'll be wanting to get back and sort yourself out for tonight. I know what you women are like.'

'Get back . . .' Jenna's mind hadn't been on practicalities. 'Like this?'

Robin put two fingers in his mouth and gave a low, distinctive whistle. A chestnut mare walked patiently into the clearing with something tucked over her withers. A grey pony was browsing on the undergrowth nearer the trees.

Robin stood up and untucked the bundle from his horse's back. Jenna realised what it was – her clothes.

'You followed me,' she stated.

'You complaining? Thought not. Here, d'you want to ride back with me? It's not that far but I've got a spare horse so you might as well. He was supposed to be lame.' He chuckled. 'But it's just an old gypsy trick.'

Pulling her dress over her head Jenna followed Robin to the edge of the clearing and watched him bend down and do something very quickly to the pony's foreleg.

'There,' he said, straightening up and patting the pony on its dappled neck. 'Sorry about that, mate. All in the course of helping something along that probably would have happened anyway. It's quite clever, really. You tie the long hairs at the back of the fetlock together in a certain way and the horse looks as though it's lame. Doesn't hurt. This old Romany fella took a shine to me at one of the festivals and explained it to me, back when I was first starting out.'

'Starting out what?'

'Starting out being me. An entrepreneur, of sorts. Rather like the birthday boy who's slipping it to you on a regular basis. Oh don't look at me like that. I can spot who's doing what to whom. Want a hand up?'

'I can manage, thanks.'

Robin went back and caught his chestnut mare. When they were both ready he began leading the way down the track.

'What was that?' Jenna asked, reining in sharply.

'What?'

'I'm sure I heard something . . . Robin, is someone following us?'

'Nothing to do with me for once if they are.' He grinned at her through his dark, clipped beard. 'And if they are, we've certainly given them something to think about. Come on. Let's get back.'

Chapter Six

HEATHER CROUCHED BEHIND a sprawling clump of elder, cursing the twig that had snapped under her foot and made the woman rider pull up and look back. No – they were moving off again. Good. Heather needed to be alone. She had too much information to digest.

She'd come three times before Alex finally let himself climax inside her. She'd thought she was going to rip apart from the sheer force of it. He'd untied her wrists and stepped back to watch – with ill-disguised amusement, she'd felt – as she'd rubbed life back into her aching limbs. Her young body felt positively raw – opened like spring earth before a new-forged plough. So much pleasure had made her feel pummelled and weak.

Nevertheless, she'd refused when Alex offered to share his horse with her again on the ride back to the Hall.

'Suit yourself,' he'd said, with no further attempt at persuasion. 'But here – take some candy. You'll need it if you're going to walk.'

Then he'd mounted, ridden off down the track and she'd soon lost sight of him.

Once dressed, Heather had walked on through the forest feeling sleepy but still erotically charged. She paid no particular attention to her path. She'd had three successive orgasms from the cock of an experienced older man. Her whole body and her whole imagination had been on fire with sex. She'd wanted all it had to give.

The forest had done something to her – the air, the very smell of it, the shifting dappled light. She'd walked, directionless, stopping now and then to rub her body against the promisingly rough bark of certain trees. She'd relished the biting textures against her nipples, even through her clothes. Or else she'd paused to rub her clitoris, through her shorts, against the little shoots and buds that were just the right height. The fabric was becoming slick with her own juice. Anyone meeting her would have been able to smell the sweet muskiness of her sex. She didn't care.

And then she'd heard his voice.

Robin was standing in a clearing, masturbating over a woman who was writhing on the ground with a snake coiled round her breasts. Heather had barely been able to keep from giving her hiding place away. A ring through his cock! If she'd thought Alex had possibilities, what could Robin teach her? She had to know.

She'd stayed hidden and watched them mount their horses afterwards. That grey one had been hers! So, Robin had thrown her and Alex together deliberately to see what happened. But she couldn't be angry. Every second of Alex's cock inside her had been a pleasure.

More disturbing had been the throwaway comment about Nick sleeping with that woman who worked for him. Still, Heather knew her brother wasn't exactly a saint. And it would serve that phoney French tart right.

She straightened up from behind the elder, brushing off the bugs that had landed on her while she'd been keeping still. She was hungry. She'd missed lunch. The chocolate bar Alex had tossed to her from his rucksack as a parting gift wasn't much help. Normally she watched what she ate – even relishing the intensity of her gnawing hunger – needing to keep her dancer's figure trim. This weekend, though, hunger kept getting the upper hand.

Pragmatism took over. Heather followed the horses' tracks back to the Hall.

Back in her room she found a packet of biscuits on the tea-making tray. They kept hunger at bay just long enough for her to shower off the stickiness of the morning's adventures – both in the saddle and out. Then her mind began to flick over other possibilities. Room service would bring her anything she fancied. Hadn't Nick told her so? Heather dialled down to the kitchens.

'Hello, room eighty-seven here. I'd like two rounds of smoked-salmon and cream cheese sandwiches with endive on wholemeal bread. And perhaps if you could ask that young waiter who arrived on the motorbike to bring it up? Oh, that's you, is it? Ten minutes. Great. Thanks.'

She hung up. So she had ten minutes to get ready. And perhaps the sandwiches would have to wait a little longer than that.

Or maybe not. One contraband pleasure before the next. She imagined eating them with him watching her. The salty intensity of the fish, its smoothness playing over her tongue. The forbidden full-fat creaminess of the cheese contrasting with the peppery crispness of the endive leaves. And the nutty, chewy texture of the fresh wholemeal bread. Sex was positively encouraged at the dance school – it helped burn off the calories. Enjoying your food was not.

Heather shrugged off her robe and rifled through the weekend bag she hadn't got round to unpacking. She had no illusions. She was nineteen, waif-like and couldn't compete with most of the women here on sheer up-front sexuality. But she could do virginal. Some men seemed to go for that.

In the end she chose a white lacy camisole, white suspender belt and ivory stockings. She pulled them on quickly, left the door ajar and got into bed, covered only by a sheet from the waist down. Very soon there was a knock.

'Come in,' she called. 'I left it open for you.'

The young waiter carried his tray into the room, put it down then paused. He looked at her lying on the bed. She thought he seemed surprised but not totally taken aback, as if this wasn't the first time a hotel guest had wanted something that wasn't strictly on the menu. Then he went to the door and deliberately locked it. When he turned back to Heather, he was already unbuttoning his waiter's uniform waistcoat and loosening his tie.

Heather flicked the sheet aside. He paused for a moment and just looked. She hadn't bothered with panties. And she was spreading her legs wide.

One hand rested casually behind her head, the other hand travelled down and parted her pink vaginal lips for him to see. The young waiter's eyes were trained on her quim. She drew her middle finger moistly over her clitoris. There was a definite bulge in his dark trousers. She didn't doubt he was ready to give her what she wanted. But there wouldn't be any harm in making him wait.

'Come here,' she ordered. 'And bring those sandwiches with you. They weren't just an excuse. I really am hungry.'

She took them, one by one, off his tray. With a deep sigh she bit into one. Food and sex – she rolled the thought indulgently round her head. The intense contrast of all the tastes and textures was everything she'd hoped for. For a second her jaw was almost paralysed with the ache of pleasure that comes from tasting piquant food when you're really, really hungry. She chewed each mouthful slowly. And she wasn't just relishing the flavours. She was relishing the look on his face as his gaze was transfixed by her bare quim, every bit as moist and delicate as the slivers of smoked fish she was slipping between her lips.

By the time one round was gone Heather's immediate hunger was satisfied and she couldn't let her other desires take a back seat any longer. She licked the very last traces of salty butter from her middle finger and sat up on the edge of the bed.

'Come closer,' she told him and he did.

She undid his belt buckle and unzipped his flies. His trousers collapsed to his ankles. Then she pulled his cotton boxer shorts down. His cock was warm and velvety. She took it in her mouth.

She'd done this before – mainly to please boyfriends who expected her to do it. But never to fruition. Not just because of the reputed calorie content but because her jaw had ached too much. And she'd never done it with this much pleasure. She became suddenly aware of what an erogenous zone the mouth could be: how literally delicious and suckable was the meat between her lips.

She lolled her tongue up and down the underside of his swelling shaft. He was groaning with excitement, even as he tugged off the last of his clothes. Heather revelled in having this much power over a man – such power to reduce him to a moaning, breathless sexual slave. She could begin to see why some women liked this so much.

His cock was alive and vital in her mouth. She could sense an extra rush of blood against her stretched lips. He was as full and hard as he could possibly be. And then, with a loud cry as a split-second warning, he ejaculated straight into the back of her throat.

Heather smiled, purringly pleased with herself, and swallowed it down. She mused on the unfamiliar taste sensation – salty and slippery like the fish. A combination she was definitely going to have to remember.

'Your turn,' she said, licking her lips.

She lay back on the bed and spread her thighs wide again. The young waiter seemed agreeably enthusiastic about the prospect of going down on her. He buried his face in her pubic hair for a moment and inhaled deeply. The ticklish sensation made her wriggle.

Can he still smell Alex on me? she wondered. Despite the shower? Does the thought of eating out a pussy so recently fucked by someone else turn him on?

He began to flick his tongue up and down her labia, burrowing and exploring the clefts between her inner and outer lips. She lay back and relaxed into his ministrations. He might have been young – scarcely older than herself perhaps – but she sensed he was going to be so, so good at this.

The tip of his tongue circled the bud of her clitoris – softly, more sensitive than any finger. He played with her hard knot of pleasure just enough – but not too much – then plunged his tongue as deep into her vagina as it would go. Like a warm and twisting snake.

After Alex's relentless thrusts this morning her quim was still fiery raw. This moist, mobile warmth was just what she needed – kissing her, kissing it all better. Heather stretched and sighed, knowing there was nothing for her to do but lie back and concentrate on receiving this young man's unstinting oral adoration.

But somehow it still wasn't enough. Something had happened to her in the forest, not just to her body but to her head. Something had been imprinted on her. And without it she couldn't come.

Heather concentrated hard. On the image of a swelling cock so different, so kinky its master had had it pierced. It was looming over her, closer and closer to her lips. It filled her world. The dappled sunlight glinted on the silver ring through its tip. It was so close now she could almost feel the metal touch her mouth – so bizarre, so beautiful. And then she felt the honeyed surge of orgasm tingle, beginning at the tops of her soft inner thighs and sweeping up right through her.

The young waiter sat back on his heels, grinning.

He looks pleased with himself, she thought. If only he knew it wasn't totally down to him . . .

'I'm still hungry,' she said out loud. 'You can fetch the rest of those sandwiches now.'

He got them and lay down beside her on the bed, feeding them to her one by one – sometimes teasing, snatching them back as she opened her mouth in anticipation.

'What's your name?' she asked eventually with half a mouthful.

'Liam,' he replied, and she realised that was the first time he'd spoken since entering the room. There was a trace of an Irish accent.

Then came a knock at the door. Heather froze in Liam's arms.

'Sis?' said Nick's voice. 'Lisette told me you'd got separated. Just wanted to check you were okay.'

'Yeah,' she replied, swallowing an awkward mouthful. 'I'm fine.'

'Right . . . You'll be ready for the treasure hunt, yeah?'

'Course I will. See you later, Nick.'

They held their breath until Nick's footsteps faded down the corridor. Then they burrowed into the pillows, giggling like naughty schoolchildren who'd just missed being caught out.

Finally Liam said, 'You noticed my bike?'

'Yes.'

'You like it? You into leather?'

'I don't know . . . yet.'

'How about I put on my biking leathers later and give it to you from behind?'

'Now you're talking!'

*

As Nick walked away down the corridor he felt uneasy. There had been something wrong with Heather's voice. God, she hadn't been crying, had she? If only he didn't feel so bloody responsible for her.

He was still mad at Lisette for riding off and leaving her in the forest. Heather was nineteen. She was sensitive. Did Lisette even remember what that was like?

His Achilles heel. His soft spot. Jenna had been right there. And that was another thing. Jenna was getting too comfortable as his mistress. That had never been the plan. She was beginning to needle him. She was trying to get inside his head. No one did that to Nick. A bit of competition – real competition, not Lisette – would pull her back into line.

So he'd keep Jenna on her toes, and leave the way clear for Heather to partner Morgan at the treasure hunt tonight – that should cheer her up. He could solve both problems at once. Nick checked his watch. Yes, there was still time to go and see Eleni.

He took the stairs two at a time and knocked on the door. The clipped, distinctive accent of someone who'd been born in Athens but educated in London replied, 'Come in.'

Nick opened the door. Eleni was wrapped in a fluffy white towel that came only halfway down her strong tanned thighs. One end was tucked into her cleavage. It was slipping a little. She made no coy attempt to hitch it up when she saw who her visitor was.

'Well, well – Nick,' she said. 'I wondered how long it would take you to get round to a little one-to-one chat.'

He leant back against the wardrobe – attempting nonchalance – and put his hands in his pockets. Also it was meant to hide the erection that had been swelling as he climbed the stairs in anticipation of seeing her. He didn't want Eleni to know just how strong an effect she had on him: not just yet. God, he was randy this weekend. Nick's appetite for sex was healthy at the best of times but at the Hall his cock was quicker than ever to respond. Must be the country air. He made a note to get out in it more often.

'I was just about to have a shower,' Eleni continued. 'Coming?'

Coming was precisely what he'd like to do. And the way she'd said it: forming the 'c' deep in her throat, rounding her lips lovingly over the vowel, closing them sensually over the 'm' – it reminded him so graphically of what she once liked to do to his cock with her mouth. His erection gave another twitch. And he was very, very tempted to follow her into the en suite bathroom without another thought for the other reason he'd come here.

'I want you to do something for me,' he said at last.

'Yeah? Textiles again? Or something a little more private and indiscreet? Let's see, how long's it been since you last fucked me, Nick? Must have been . . . ooh, around the time you went off to chase that has-been French woman. Not that I bear a grudge.'

'Neither,' he replied with difficulty. 'I want you to stop distracting Morgan Heselton with your rather unfair advantages.'

'Why's that? Got an interest in him yourself? Broadening your horizons, Nick? I warn you, I don't think he's your type.'

Nick forced his jaw to relax. He hadn't realised

he'd begun to clench it. He found himself remembering just why his affair with Eleni had been so fiery. Why Lisette's Parisian coolness had actually come as a relief. And why his subsequent bedmates, like Jenna, had tended towards the compliant.

'No,' he said. 'You know damn well where my tastes lie. But Heselton's here for a reason. He runs a dance troupe my sister's keen to get into. Don't distract him. Give him some space.'

'You want him to fuck her?'

Nick's jaw tightened again. He didn't like to think of Heather having sex. 'I want him to notice her.'

'I'm not stopping her. If she wants to come and have a go at him she's quite welcome. I don't always like an easy ride. But who would you put your money on, Nick? Unless of course . . . someone else distracted me instead. You know I'm sentimental underneath. Something for old time's sake? And Nick, take your hands out of your pockets. I know you only ever slouch like that when you're trying to hide a stiffy. See – you can't fool me. You haven't really changed a bit.'

Nick took his hands out of his pockets and held them in the air, grinning. Left to itself, his erection tented out the front of his loose, casual trousers. He could sense Eleni's gaze fix hungrily on it. For all her infuriating petulance, she really was addicted to cock.

It was, he thought wryly, one of those win-win situations that management-theory courses go on about. Not that he'd ever had much time for any of that psychobabble. And Eleni was right. She didn't always like an easy ride.

'You mentioned a shower,' he said. 'Lead the way.'

They went into the bathroom. The shower was above the old-fashioned bath, not in a cubicle on its own. Plenty of room for two, he thought with satisfaction. Plenty of room for games.

Eleni turned to face him, unwrapped her towel, dropped it on the floor and spread her arms wide. Nick grinned. Her absolute and thoroughly non-Anglo Saxon confidence in her voluptuous body had always been one of the things he'd enjoyed.

'Well,' she said, 'what do you think?'

'I think you've put on a bit of weight in the last few years. But definitely in the right places.'

She grinned mischievously and cupped and lifted her big breasts.

'You mean these have got bouncier? Yes, I thought so. Ah – no,' she continued as Nick reached for them himself. 'I've got a head start on you. Better catch me up.'

She turned and stepped quickly under the shower, letting the water run warmly over her body. For a moment Nick stood, mesmerised by the way the rivulets ski-jumped from the berry-ripe tips of her dark, protruding nipples. Then he realised what she'd meant. He undressed quickly, dropped his clothes on the bathroom floor and joined her under the pounding water. He fastened his mouth on hers, thrust his tongue deeply inside and crushed her intensely female naked body against his.

They soaped each other generously all over. The frothy white lather was paler than Eleni's Mediterranean skin. He covered her breasts in it. White and slippery, they were even more of a turn-on for him than ever. He fondled them roughly and they seemed to slide out of his hands with a life of their own. But he left her nipples unsoaped. They were the longest, darkest, most outrageously erectile nipples of any woman he'd ever known. The contrast between their rich, coffee-caramel colour and the whiteness of the lather fascinated him.

She smothered his penis in creamy suds. As her hands slid up and down his shaft, the lubrication made her fingers feel silkier than ever. His cock was so high and bursting and her slithery touch so mind-blowingly erotic that he wondered several times whether he'd already climaxed and it was his own semen she was massaging into his cock. But no, his balls were still tight and bursting. They weren't to have their release just yet. Eleni gave a last slippery glide to his tortured penis, then pressed herself into his arms.

For a few moments they writhed their seal-slick bodies against one another, belly to soapy belly. Her breasts were squashed deliciously against his rib cage; he loved the feeling of that. It reminded him of the times, long past, when he'd make her lie on the bed beneath him so he could kneel astride her and wank furiously all over her breasts. Then he would lie on top of her and rub his cock cream into her body with his. Would they do that again this afternoon? Time-wise, he really could only afford to come once with Eleni. And choosing between the possibilities was the most delectable torture.

They let the shower wash the suds off them then. Eleni stepped back out of the jet of water, knelt down and took Nick's cock fully in her mouth.

He gasped and groaned. Never, since leaving Eleni to pursue Lisette, had he found a lover so adept or so enthusiastic about deep throat. Most women balked at it. For Eleni, it was a matter of pride. And so often she'd taunted and challenged him with her words that symbolically it was one hell of a turn on for him to literally gag her with his prick. Nick buried his fingers in her thick, dark hair and pressed his groin hard up to her nose and mouth.

He longed to come right at the back of her throat. Like he'd done so many times when they were younger. But he'd have the chance – later. His libido was on a rising tide. Even Jenna and Lisette together weren't enough for him any more. From now on, whenever Eleni was in the country, he'd make a point of seeking her out.

But this time – the first time after so many years – it had to be a simple, animal fuck. He needed to remind her just how roughly he could satisfy a woman.

Reluctantly, then, he withdrew from her mouth. 'I've got other plans. On the bed.'

They dried themselves urgently. Both their bodies were still a little damp when they went through to the bedroom. Eleni lay back on the double bed and spread her legs wide – wide enough so he got the best possible view of her glistening, dark-lipped sex. She seemed to remember this old game they used to play.

'Beg for it,' Nick ordered her.

'Come and fuck me, lover. Please. I'm ready. I've missed you. I want it so badly.'

'What do you want?'

'I want you to thrust that horny great big prick into my juicy pussy. Look, you can see how juicy it is.' Here, she began stroking her vaginal lips and clitoris. They were clean, fresh from the shower and slippery with her own clear honey. 'See how much I want you.'

'Why is it my cock you want?'

'Because it's so thick. It's so horny and always

ready. I know you only have to look at me and it goes hard. I've never known a man as horny for me as you. You know how much of a turn on that is for a woman? Come here. Come here and use it on me.'

'What have you been doing while I've been away?'

'Every night I lie in bed and feel my tits. I imagine it's your hands on them. I know how much you love them. I pinch my nipples hard and wish it was your mouth sucking them – but of course it's not as good. I rub my pussy. I see how many fingers I can get inside me but it's not the same. Only your beautiful prick will do, lover. I need to feel you explode as you come.'

'You're not fooling anyone. I know how many other men have had their cocks in there.'

'Oh yes, Nick, but none as horny as you. They were all so refined. They made love – as they called it – with the lights low and saying nothing. They wouldn't talk dirty like you. You've spoiled me for any other man. Only you can stretch me enough now. Only you feel like a bomb going off inside me. Please, please fuck me. Don't make me wait.'

Eleni was writhing uncontrollably on the bed now – still with her legs spread wide and still with her fingers working wildly at her clitoris.

'Hurry up, Nick. I so want to come. If you don't fuck me soon I might wank myself to it – I might not be able to stop. And I don't want that. I want to come with your prick inside me.'

She was bucking her hips and offering up the most inviting view. Their eyes met. Nick read genuine fear there now – fear he'd been teasing and was going to walk away and leave her unsatisfied after all. Yes, he'd pushed her just the right amount this time. She was truly ready.

With a whoop of triumph Nick bounced on to the bed and mounted her. Eleni's eyes widened in genuine shock at the speed with which he thrust his penis home. Nick began to fuck her roughly and in earnest.

Eleni always had been the sort of woman who came quickly – and loudly – no matter what he did to her. He'd never had to worry about her satisfaction. In fact, the rougher and more selfish he was the more she seemed to like it. He'd often wondered if she was 'difficult' purely to provoke him and make him act this way with her. Now, as he grabbed a large breast in each hand to increase his arousal, he wondered for the first time if Jenna's recent 'uppity' behaviour couldn't be schooled into similar channels . . . But no. He rather enjoyed the contrast. And he intended to enjoy Eleni. Again. Very soon.

Beneath him she was flailing and moaning and telling him he had the biggest, best cock that had ever fucked her. He loved hearing that. Of course it was true.

He couldn't have held himself back even if he'd wanted to. A wave went through his balls and lower belly. It rippled all along the straining shaft of his cock. He was coming into her and it seemed as if he would go on coming for ever.

He stayed inside her for a few minutes afterwards, enjoying the warmth and snug fit of her quim. Eleni smiled up at him. It was an unforced, uncalculated smile. He was sure of that.

'There's a lot to be said for revisiting old lovers,' she whispered. 'Do that to me again and I'll steer well clear of Morgan Heselton.'

'Funny – I was thinking along the same lines

myself. I'm damn sure my libido can cope with giving it to three women. When you're next in the UK, look me up.'

'Let me suck you off now, Nick. You know I can get you hard again. And you know how much I love sucking cock.'

God, he was tempted. But there was Jenna – and tonight. Just how many ejaculations in a row could he expect from a cock on the eve of its thirtieth birthday? Admittedly this place seemed to be having an amazing effect on his sex drive but even so, he didn't want to push it.

'I can't.' He glanced pointedly at his watch. 'I need to be getting ready for this evening.'

'Later then? We're supposed to be having a treasure hunt, aren't we? We could easily sneak off somewhere and I could suck you off.'

'Sorry, I've already made . . . arrangements.'

'Who is she? If I like the look of her, we could make it a threesome.'

Nick withdrew from her abruptly and rolled away across the bed. 'I don't do threesomes. You know that.'

'Oh, Nick, I thought you'd have grown out of that by now.' Then her voice changed. It was no longer wheedling but back to peppery. 'Oh yes, poor little Nick who was so traumatised when he walked into his parents' bedroom one afternoon and found his father and uncle indulging in a bit of free love with his uncle's wife.'

Nick went cold. He remembered. He'd been out with his mother on a Christmas shopping trip. They'd arrived home earlier than expected. He'd heard noises in the bedroom. Maybe the dog was trapped in there. He'd gone to let her out. But it hadn't been the dog.

It had been Daddy and Uncle Martin and Auntie Faye all lying on the bed. They hadn't even heard anyone come in. Auntie Faye had been lying in the middle on her back, eyes closed, moaning. The brothers had been lying either side of her. Each had his mouth clamped on one – it had seemed to Nick at the time – impossibly huge breast. Their cocks had been bigger and harder than Nick had ever imagined a cock could grow.

He'd stood frozen to the spot. He'd shouted, 'Mum!' and she'd come running. The threesome on the bed had realised they'd been caught. There wasn't any point in explaining or pretending. Nick's mum had seen what he'd seen and that had been the end of everything normal and cosy for him.

He'd met Eleni at business school when he was still too young. Too raw. Too trusting. He shouldn't have told her anything that gave her a handle on him. And when that mouth wasn't sucking cock it had a tendency to gossip.

'Yeah, well,' he finished for her, 'traumatised me so much I had to grow up and make obscene amounts of money to get the smell of joss sticks out of my head for good. So don't knock it, right?'

Chapter Seven

NICK HAD ORDERED dinner to be early that evening – and nothing too heavy. There would be another midnight buffet if guests still felt in need of something before bed. But for now he didn't want them weighed down or bloated. They should be free to enter into the spirit of the game. That was important to him.

When he judged the time was right, Nick stood up and tapped his fork on his wine glass for attention. And how quickly he got it. Conversation faded and the whole room turned to look at him. That in itself sent the blood rushing to his groin.

There didn't seem to be a consensus among the party as to whether 'fancy dress' rules still applied, which amused him. Sure, flowing dresses – medieval or Victorian – weren't exactly appropriate for searching the woods at night, but he'd enjoyed the way they scooped low over the women's breasts and the way the corsets thrust their curves up for his approval. He was pleased to note that several women were still wearing them. Eleni, of course, was still in costume – not that there was very much of hers to snag on anything. She caught his eye across the room and winked. He deliberately showed no sign of understanding her.

Nick himself was still dressed as a well-to-do Italian Renaissance man. He felt it suited him – the first modern capitalists. And he liked the women's curious glances at his thigh-clasping breeches and well-formed codpiece. He was particularly pleased with the codpiece. It gave him the look of a permanent hard on and at the same time disguised when he was really beginning to get one. Like right now.

When absolute hush had dominated the hall for at least ten seconds (how he loved to keep them waiting!) Nick spoke.

'You're all aware by now that tonight's entertainments kick off with a treasure hunt. And the treasure at the end of it is this.'

He held up a photograph.

'A unique, one-off reproduction of an Anglo Saxon amber necklace found on an archaeological dig not far from here. I'm sure I don't have to tell you just how winnable that is. Whether you work on your own, in couples or in groups is entirely up to you. The waitresses will be coming round in a minute to hand out the first set of clues. Good luck, everyone.'

As he sat down again, the twin redheads moved among the tables with baskets of small, crisp envelopes, handing them out as they went. At least those girls were still in medieval costume, Nick thought. His palms itched as he enjoyed the sight of their plump breasts when they bent to hand out clues to the people nearest him.

One girl reached past him to give an envelope to Lisette, seated on his left. As she did so the straining linen of her bodice slipped a little more and he caught a momentary glimpse of something nestling at her cleavage – a birthmark, perhaps? That would be one way of telling the twins apart, he supposed. Nick mulled over his promise to himself concerning those two redheads. He just hoped he'd have the time.

It didn't take long for the banqueting hall to empty. Even desserts were left half finished and glasses of good claret half drunk. No one seemed to want anyone else to have a head start. Nick was pleased. He could smell avarice. He understood that.

He followed, although he wouldn't be taking part. Jenna was walking just in front of him, clutching an envelope and a torch, like most of the others. She'd abandoned her costume, he noticed, but the way her light summer dress swished over her hips as she walked breathed life into his hidden, fading erection. And there was the distinct possibility she wasn't wearing panties.

As they passed the dark Victorian conservatory he caught up with her, clasped her arm and drew her into the shadows. It amused – and gratified – him that she glanced about once or twice to make sure there were no silent observers this time around.

'Not you,' he whispered, plucking the envelope out of her hand. 'I told you I've got other plans for us tonight.'

Jenna looked petulant. 'I don't get a chance to find the treasure? I rather liked it.'

'I'll get you another one if it's that important.'

'Another one? But you said . . .'

'Yeah, yeah, that it was a unique one-off reproduction. So I told a little white lie to sell folks an idea and make them enjoy the fun and games even more. What's new?'

Jenna was looking hard at him. He couldn't be quite sure what she was thinking but he knew he didn't like that look. Nick grinned and slipped a hand up her mid-thigh-length skirt. That was always a good way to get her out of a sulky mood. Oh, he'd been right. She wasn't wearing anything underneath. His right hand cupped one cool cheek of her ass and squeezed.

'Meet me in the boathouse,' he said. 'You know where it is – at the far end of the lake. I've made sure the clues direct everyone well away from there.' He noticed she was wearing a watch. He wasn't, but he was pretty good at estimating time. 'See you in about ten minutes.'

He withdrew his hand and gave her a playful but proprietorial slap on the rump. 'Best we're not seen obviously going there together,' he finished. 'You first.'

Obediently Jenna slipped out and joined the throng of people who were still milling past in the bright corridor. He wasn't totally taken in by her compliance, though. There was something about Jenna, something that had only begun to show itself this weekend. Sure, she was still keen enough to please him sexually. It was something else – something less easy for him to put his finger on. She wasn't quite where he wanted her to be.

Nick wondered if it had been a mistake to direct quite everyone away from the boathouse. Perhaps if he'd arranged things differently. Perhaps if he could have timed it so Jenna walked in and found him with Eleni. Oh, nothing too overtly sexual. Nothing Jenna could throw a fit about. Just enough to raise her suspicions that, given another five minutes, she might have walked in and found Eleni on her knees with his cock deep, deep in her mouth. He knew damn well that since he'd dropped it into the conversation, Jenna was haunted by images like that.

Nick shrugged. Oh well, not this time. But there was still plenty of the weekend left.

Jenna paused by the spreading, twisted magnolia tree in the middle of the dark lawns. She could see the boathouse from here but she was sure the leaves masked her shape. Ten minutes Nick had said – a quarter of an hour ago. She deliberately wasn't hurrying. Why should she? Of course she was going to go to the boathouse. Of course she was going to meet him. Her vulva, bare to the evening air, tightened involuntarily at the thought. And no doubt they'd have all the more explosive sex for being infuriated at each one keeping the other waiting. Nick played power waiting games. No reason why she shouldn't, too.

'Thought you'd given me the slip for a moment there.'

Jenna whipped round. But even in the dark she could tell it wasn't Nick. Lights from the faraway Hall glinted on a single earring and the face silhouetted behind her had a short, clipped beard.

'Robin . . . I'm supposed to be meeting Nick.'

'Doesn't take a genius to work that one out. Where?'

'The boathouse.'

'Right. I'll find someone to tell him you've been . . . waylaid.'

He was twisting something in his hands. She realised it was a black silk scarf.

'Blindfold,' he explained. 'Essential for a really authentic kidnap. And you are being kidnapped, Jenna.'

'I don't understand ... Is this part of tonight's entertainment plan?'

'Depends whose plan you're working to.'

A second figure appeared behind Robin. Jenna recognised him: a young man who'd served them dinner that night. She remembered him having a faint Irish accent.

'The treasure isn't where Nick thinks it is,' Robin continued. 'I moved it. And tampered with some of the clues – only some of them. It should be chaos.'

'Why? What are you getting out of this?'

He laughed. 'A great deal of ... satisfaction. Don't you know? I can't help it. Robin Goodfellow and all that – the eternal prankster. But none of that need concern you. You're off on another adventure.'

He wrapped the blindfold round her eyes. He wound it securely several times round her head before tying it off. Even if she'd opened her eyes beneath it, even if it hadn't already been dark, she really wouldn't have been able to see a thing.

'Somehow,' Robin murmured, 'you still don't look like you've been properly kidnapped. Let me see ...'

He began to unbutton her flimsy summer dress. It slipped readily off her shoulders, leaving her completely naked. Even though Jenna was blindfolded she was profoundly aware of the two men scrutinising her nude form. She felt her skin tingling under their gaze. Her breasts in particular felt acutely exposed. She expected one or other of the men to cup and fondle them. In fact she was ready for it. She stood there stiffly waiting for the touch of a firm hand or a flick of a tongue at her nipple. None came. Anticipation was driving her crazy.

'Liam,' Robin began at last, 'could I trouble you for the – er – accoutrements? Thank you.'

Jenna felt something being slipped around her neck. It was cool. It weighed heavily on her collar-bones – like a metal collar. Then she felt something similar being fitted to each wrist. Finally one of the men – she wasn't sure which – bent down between her legs and, with a slight clink of chains, snapped something around each ankle. She had a fair idea what they were. Some sort of hobble which would allow her to walk but not to run.

'Do you know,' she heard Robin's voice again, 'I think a woman looks almost unbearably sexy wearing nothing but a set of restraints. Come on. Time to go and start the real party.'

She heard another light metallic clink and there was a tug on her collar. She was being pulled along on a lead. The hobbles meant she was restricted to tiny, mincing steps. The feel of the night air changed on her naked skin. They were moving out of the shelter of the magnolia tree. Hands on her shoulders spun her round until her sense of direction – never that good – was lost. They were moving forwards again – but she had no idea where 'forwards' was.

For all she knew Robin could be parading her past a silent line of male treasure hunters. They'd like that. Treganza Leisure's bright young marketing executive, Nick's 'bit on the side' (she didn't share his conviction that their affair was a well-kept secret) exposed for anyone to get an eyeful. Taken down a peg or two: she was sure many in the company would like to see that. Anyone could be staring at her bare ass, her bush, her breasts as they jiggled in time to her restricted walk. She'd never know. It had all the elements of fantasy. And the thought made her labia moist as they rubbed together with her short, mincing steps.

They stopped for a moment. She heard Robin say something to someone. She couldn't make out many of the words but was sure she'd caught 'the boathouse'. There was the sound of high feminine laughter. Then another tug on her collar and they were on their way again.

The air smelled different now – similar to the afternoon's freshness but heightened with after-dark moistness. And things crunched and crackled beneath her sandals. Robin was leading her into the wood. The wood – wasn't that where Nick had hinted most of the treasure hunt was going to take place? How much *had* Robin disrupted it? Not enough, perhaps. There would still be people searching among the trees. Had Robin brought her here, chained and blindfolded, to put her on display?

They stopped for the last time. Hands guided her down. She was at an angle of about forty-five degrees. She felt she must be leaning on a tree, either partially fallen or growing at an angle to the ground. It had a thick bole. She straddled it like a horse and heard a click in front of her as if her wrist restraints were being locked together on the far side of the trunk.

The bark was rough and knobbly against her naked skin. She ground her pubis experimentally against it to see if she could give herself sexual pleasure. She could. Enough to reach orgasm? Maybe she'd find out.

Her heavy breasts had splayed out on either side of the trunk. Then she felt a soft moistness nuzzle her. At last! A warm, eager tongue circling her nipple – flicking, teasing. But only the very tip of the tongue. She couldn't tell – though she was desperate to know – if the mouth it emerged from was surrounded by a springy, clipped beard.

And then someone started on the other breast. Jenna moaned. This was her idea of erotic heaven: to have both highly sensitive nipples sucked at once. Two men sharing her, both driven mad by desire for her magnificent breasts. She didn't care what else they did to her. She didn't care that her bare ass was exposed to the night air for any passing stranger to see. All she cared about was the double stimulation she was getting from two men's tongues.

After a long time one of the mouths went away. She moaned a complaint but it wasn't heeded. After all, she was a captive. She had no say. There was a rustle of movement and a sound like flies being unzipped. Then one hand parted the cheeks of her ass and a finger dipped into her quim as if testing the water.

She was very, very wet. The finger slipped easily between her labia and covered her stretched perineum with her own slippery juice before burrowing deep again.

The tongue at her nipple was still pleasuring her as frantically as ever. A hand cupped her other breast, rolling and pinching. It was almost as good as mouth-work, though not quite. Not quite as warm and mobile. She rubbed her pubis against the tree trunk again, giving the hidden bud of her clitoris a diffuse stimulation. Why wasn't anything else happening yet?

From the sound she'd heard, she was sure the man behind her had unzipped his flies. She didn't doubt he had an erection. Why were they waiting?

It began to dawn on her. Even though she was blindfolded and restrained, they still wanted something more from her. A final, unequivocal sign of her submission.

'One of you fuck me,' she moaned. 'I don't care which one it is. One of you get his great horny hard on and stick it in my pussy.'

As soon as she'd said it she was penetrated from behind.

She'd said, 'I don't care which one it is,' but that wasn't strictly true. As the man behind thrust into her, she began to wonder – what would it be like being fucked by a cock whose tip was pierced?

Was it happening now? She tightened her vaginal muscles against him, trying to slow his thrusts. What would a thick ring feel like against her most sensitive inner flesh? Or did he take it out for full, penetrative sex? Could she feel a difference now? She wasn't sure.

Images of Robin's pierced cock filled her head. Cock, cock, cock, she silently repeated, loving the word, the erotic charge it gave her. The memory of him coming in a white arc over her breasts as she'd writhed on the ground beneath him that afternoon. The fantasy of him nestling it deep in her cleavage and rubbing it up and down, the chunky metal gliding between her breasts. Taking it in her mouth, running her tongue up and down that ring, exploring the places where it entered his flesh, finding out if it really was different. Robin fucking her wildly as perhaps – just perhaps – he was doing now. It was when she went a step further and imagined the pierced cock buggering her ass that a sudden, jolting orgasm wracked her body.

The man behind her speeded up. His ramrod-stiff prick fucked her without finesse or mercy. She couldn't believe he could keep going for so long. She loved the feel of it, to be able to relax and simply enjoy the furious friction. Still she agonised over just what she could feel. And then there was that telltale full-to-bursting moment and, a split second later, a deep groan from behind her as he came.

He didn't withdraw immediately. Then she heard Robin's voice in front of her and her fantasies were dashed.

'Take off her blindfold, Liam. Only good manners to let a lady know who's just fucked her.'

The silk scarf was unwound. She blinked a couple of times as the dark world came into focus and she saw Robin leaning against the tree by her head, looking amused.

'You bastard,' she told him. 'You knew damn well ... Why didn't you ... ?'

'Ah, but that's not what you said, Jenna. You really do need to be specific. I would have thought someone who uses words to make her living would have appreciated that. Never mind. You've come to a good teacher.'

Chapter Eight

IN THE BOATHOUSE Nick reached for his Rolex watch to press the button and illuminate the dial. But it wasn't there. Then he remembered leaving it on his dressing table. Too twenty-first century. Mere practicalities weren't going to spoil his look.

Still, it felt as if he'd been here for ages. The candles he'd brought with him had started to burn down. What the hell was Jenna playing at? He'd teach her to play games and keep him waiting like this. Because that's what she was doing, he knew it. She was needling him again. Trying to prove something. Nobody did that to Nick – especially not a girl he'd plucked from relative obscurity and turned into someone whose name appeared in glossy, leisure-trade magazines every other month. When Jenna got here . . .

Nick's cock went hard again as he worked out what he'd do. He might have been – and frequently was – the dominant partner in bed. But he'd never been *that* dominant. He'd never tried to break her will, dent her pleasure, keep her dancing to his tune for hours and hours and hours. He'd never brought his hand down hard on that tempting white ass. To be honest he hadn't really thought about it before. It had never been his thing. But tonight, suddenly, he had the urge. And if Jenna didn't like the consequences of her games, she shouldn't have started to play them.

The blood pounded through the taut veins in his cock as he imagined putting Jenna over his knee and spanking her roughly till she begged for mercy. He'd gone hard and soft so many times while waiting for her, his cock was beginning to ache. The urge to touch himself was overwhelming. He longed to take it out and masturbate. Hell, why shouldn't he? Serve Jenna right if she turned up and found things weren't ready and waiting for her. She'd have to coax him into another erection. He'd make her go down on him and suck till her jaw ached and he was hard again.

Nick sat down on one of the many rugs he'd ordered to be brought here. With a sigh, he removed the ornate, embroidered Renaissance codpiece and set his impatient manhood free. He began to stroke it slowly and lovingly. Nick knew damn well he could bed virtually any woman he wanted. He was young, athletic, sexy and the size of his fortune alone got the juice running between so many women's thighs. But still, he thought, sometimes he just wanted a good, straightforward wank. He was proud of his cock: its size, its responsiveness, its solid weight in his hand. He rubbed firmly, all the way from the base of his shaft to its swollen head, knowing that very soon his jet of thick white sperm would arc and splatter over the boathouse floor.

Then the door opened. Nick sat bolt upright. 'About bloody time—' he began, but it wasn't Jenna standing in the doorway.

The redheads giggled and nudged each other. They seemed amused – but not surprised – to find him that way.

And suddenly Nick wasn't sure which was worse – to have them burst in unexpectedly and discover him wanking or to have them looking on while his erection rapidly deflated as it was doing now.

The girls exchanged glances again. Then one of them bobbed a fake curtsey and said, 'Begging your pardon, sir, but we've been sent to tell you the lady you're waiting for has been waylaid by bandits.'

Just what the hell was happening? None of this was in the plan. Nick's sudden anger had its usual side effect. His penis twitched back into life – much to the girls' undisguised amusement.

'Look,' he began, 'I'd appreciate it – I mean I'd really, *really* appreciate it – if you didn't mention to anyone you found me like this. I'll make it worth your while. What d'you want – a bonus? I'll see you get it, no problem. Off the record. Cash.'

Again they exchanged looks in that maddening way of theirs as if words were something they didn't need. Then the one slightly nearer the boathouse door closed it firmly behind her.

'I think,' she said, 'we can make things a little more interesting than that.'

In perfect synchronicity they began to unlace their bodices. Nick's reviving cock grew harder. This was what he'd been fantasising about since the previous evening: seeing those voluptuous, freckled breasts fully on display. A tiny nagging voice at the back of his head told him this was shaping up to be a three-some, and that he knew what threesomes meant ... But the thunder of his pulse drummed it out. And anyway, perhaps it was time to lay that particular ghost?

The two waitresses were standing topless before him. But what Nick saw made him take in a sharp breath.

'Which do you prefer?' said one of them. 'Natural or pierced?'

Naked, there was definitely a way to tell the girls apart. Sure, both had the same exaggerated hourglass figures, both the same thick auburn hair, both the same highly touchable freckle-dusted skin. But one of them had pierced nipples sporting delicate gold rings – you could only just see them in the candlelight. And something else besides.

Part of Nick was fascinated. The piercings made her nipples stand out, pouting in a way he'd never seen before. They drew attention to themselves outrageously. He was so, so tempted to find out what they'd feel like in his mouth. But, damn it, the dark shape he'd noticed earlier at dinner wasn't a birth mark. It was the edge of a tattoo. A snake curved itself sinuously over one breast and under the other. And, while a couple of girls as well-endowed as this might just talk him out of his reservations about troilism, snakes were a different matter.

'Definitely unpierced,' he told them.

The girls swapped looks, shrugged, nodded, then went into action.

One girl – the unpierced one – came and stood over him. She leant forwards a little, offering her heavy breasts to his face and hands. Nick was in heaven. He cupped her big, freckled hemispheres, assuring himself that her skin was really as soft and as irresistible to fondle as he'd believed. After playing and jiggling with them he squeezed her breasts together and buried his face in her deep, deep cleavage. Locker-room, nudging wisdom had always told him there was something different about the scent of a natural redhead. He could believe it now. There was something. Something unexpectedly mossy and green.

Then the pierced twin crawled between her sister's legs and began ministering to Nick's cock. At first she only pursed her lips and blew on it, round and round the aching head, up and down the shaft. It was divinely sensual, but at the same time it drove Nick crazy. He wanted to come. He desperately needed to come and his poor cock was so confused by the evening's false starts, it was going to need some good rough handling to climax.

The twin on top, who'd been pressing her breasts into his face, drew back slightly. He seized one of her nipples in his mouth and tongued her for all he was worth. And the way she began to moan was so satisfying.

Then the twin who was on her knees took him fully in her mouth. Christ, he'd thought Eleni was good at sucking a man off! This girl had a tongue that never ceased – always working on him, milking him, never in the same place for more than a second. And apparently never tiring. How many men had she taken between her mobile lips to get that good? Nick almost came just at the thought of it.

He was about to come anyway. The familiar tightening, the telltale build up of tension in his balls. But just before the moment of ejaculation his fellatrix seized the base of his shaft and squeezed. His orgasm was put on hold. His erection even wilted a little.

Then her furious tongue went back to work, making his cock an iron bar again.

He lost count of the number of times she did that. He wouldn't have believed his cock could have coped with such torture and still gone on rising to the challenge. But it did. He was fascinated by what she was doing to him. So fascinated he almost forgot about the twin on top whose breasts were dangling in his face – and that was unheard of for Nick.

Then finally the twin below did something different. Her long drawn out, sweet torture of his cock had produced plenty of lubricating fluid. She rubbed her fingertip over his glans until it was well coated in the clear, slippery juice. Then she slid her fingertip into his ass while she continued to suck.

She touched a trigger point and Nick came in an explosion with all the force of the pent-up orgasms she'd made him hold back. His ejaculation seemed to last for ever. He imagined himself pumping gallons of sperm into her mouth and she swallowed it all down.

At that moment, while warm waves of pleasure were still coursing down his penis, the twin on top pressed her breasts aggressively into his face. He couldn't breathe. They were so soft, so malleable, so all-enveloping. Nick felt his head spin. He was on the point of passing out. But what a way to go . . .

The girls drew back and left Nick panting. They glanced at each other and smiled again – unreadable smiles. Then they began to put on their dresses and lace up their bodices and all Nick could do was gasp like a stranded fish.

He realised they had had him completely in their power for a while. He wasn't used to that. And there had been three of them. A different balance, true, but he hadn't thought about his father, aunt and uncle once. Perhaps his hang-up was really gone. Perhaps he could begin to explore new possibilities.

The twins were turning to go. Dressed, he could no longer tell them apart. The delicate nipple rings didn't show through the heavy brocade of her bodice. He knew he'd be eyeing up their breasts more intently than ever from now on, for the delicious challenge of trying to work out which twin was which.

One of them opened the door, then paused and looked back. 'You mentioned before that you'd make it worth our while to keep quiet about a certain thing. I reckon the stakes are higher now. We don't want cash. But we'll be round sometime this weekend to collect. Expect us when you see us.'

They closed the boathouse door behind them. Nick was alone. 'Collect?' He was looking forward to it already.

Lisette stumbled as a bramble her torch hadn't picked out caught her across the shin. She hitched up her Heroine of the Bastille dress and cursed herself for staying in fancy dress tonight when so many of the others had forsaken it for something more practical. And where the hell was she anyway? There were no other guests in sight or earshot. If she'd been conned she couldn't work out why.

It had happened just as she'd been leaving the banqueting hall. Robin had caught her arm and drawn her aside.

'I haven't forgiven you, you know,' she'd snapped before he'd had a chance to speak.

'For what?'

'This morning on the ride. Pissing off and leaving us. I ended up losing the other two as well.'

'Ah. That.'

Robin grinned. His teeth were very white against his dark beard. And the front two were slightly crooked. Someone like Nick would have had them expensively straightened long ago. It made him look boyish. And difficult to stay angry with.

She'd never found out what had happened to Alex and Heather. Alex hadn't volunteered anything. She strongly suspected he hadn't been able to keep his hands off such a fresh-faced little ingénue at close quarters and had slipped off into the woods to give her a fuck.

If he had she wished he wouldn't be so secretive about it. They had no exclusive claims on each other – they'd long ago agreed that. And she'd often thought a damn good shafting would stop Heather wandering around like a sleepwalker.

The thought of delicate Heather coming up against a Texan bull like Alex made her want to laugh out loud. If he had given her one – and she was really beginning to hope that he had – she wanted to hear the details. *All* the details. How she had responded. How Alex had felt when he thrust his horny old cock into her tight quim. Or wherever. It could be an interesting prelude to their next passionate fuck. Later she'd insist he gave her a full account.

Robin was speaking to her again. 'The treasure's not buried where Nick thinks it is any more. You might find these instructions more to your tastes.'

So she'd been following the clues for . . . how long? She'd lost track of when she'd started. Long enough, though. Long enough to set her wondering if Robin was playing some sort of game whose rules she hadn't sussed.

Then she saw them through the trees. Lights. Nothing to do with the Hall or its outbuildings. These were dancing and flickering. They had to be flaming torches. The clue in her hand at last made sense. She headed towards the lights.

Lisette found herself on the edge of a clearing. She had no way of knowing how roundabout a route she'd taken to get here or how far away she was from the Hall. Several braziers crackled in a circle near the centre of the clearing. Some medieval-style tents stood in the shadows beyond. Then she saw the pale image on the ground. Was it glowing? She flicked off her torch. Yes, it was definitely glowing. If it had been painted, then someone had used fluorescent paint.

It was beautiful. The naked body of a man topped by a lion's head. His cock was huge and pointed straight up against his belly. She knew that was where the answer lay.

Lisette walked forwards to stand at the image's feet. She was sure the treasure must be buried beneath the giant cock. But how could she dig it up and disturb the outline of something so powerful, so beautiful? Then, in the wavering firelight, she noticed a patch of leaf litter some inches from the tip of the lion-man's foreskin, like the splash of an ejaculation. It looked as if it might have been recently disturbed. She knelt and brushed the loose debris away. The necklace was hidden not very far beneath.

She held it up to the firelight. Fire was absolutely right for the honeyed amber beads in their heavy gold settings. The flames moved within them, making them look liquid. She rubbed the beads against her lips. They had the strange, tactile warmth that only amber has. She loved it. It was hers. The feminine thrill of acquisition tingled through her.

Lisette was a very wealthy woman who still held the majority shareholding in Treganza International. But owning new and beautiful things had never lost its novelty. She smoothed the leaf litter back into place on the giant's belly and, in gratitude, bent to kiss his cock.

The taste surprised her. There was a saltiness in the white outlines, like real semen. Although she knew it was impossible, she wanted to take him in her mouth. If she worshipped this sexual, animal god with her fellating tongue, how violently would he come? How long for? How many gallons of semen would he pump down her throat?

There was a snap of dry twigs behind her.

'Lie down,' commanded a voice she recognised.

To be honest, Heather had never had that much interest in the treasure hunt. It wasn't her sort of thing. And as for fun and games in the woods, hadn't she done that already today? Getting back to nature was all well and good, but her curiosity itched. She was intent on other possibilities.

So, when the woman dressed as Cleopatra whispered in her ear as they were leaving the Hall, Heather relished the rare opportunity to be one step ahead.

'Look,' Eleni said, 'Morgan just asked me to be his partner for the treasure hunt. But I made a deal. I know it's important for you two to – ah – talk business. If you want me to make some excuse . . .'

Heather stopped, turned and looked at the other woman. Eleni was older and exuded a sexuality you could almost touch. Her costume displayed as much of her voluptuous brown body as it possibly could. And yet Heather felt she suddenly had the advantage over her.

'No, it's okay,' she replied. 'I've got other unfinished business myself. You go ahead. Have fun.'

Eleni looked at her strangely, appeared to be on the point of arguing but then changed her mind and lost herself in the crowd leaving the Hall.

Heather turned back against the flow of people and headed for the dining room. She wasn't doing what Nick wanted her to do. And it felt fun.

She didn't find who she was looking for, though. Not in the banqueting hall. Not among the staff clearing up in the kitchens. Not even in reception or loitering in the corridors. After more than an hour she decided to try the old converted stable block where she'd seen his bike pull up.

The powerful Kawasaki was parked directly beneath a high watt security light. But there was no sign of Liam. Heather walked up to the bike and stroked the saddle.

Black leather. She'd had enough of being elfin and decided that when she got back to London she was going to augment her wardrobe with lots it. After all, if you were after those sort of clothes, London had to be the place to get them. And she was sure she could get Nick to pay off her credit card. Again.

A soft Irish voice behind her said, 'You decided you're into leather?'

Heather whipped round. 'I was looking for you. Where have you been?'

'I'm sorry, I didn't think we'd arranged anything. I was busy.'

She took in Liam's ruffled hair, the button undone on his shirt, the fact that his flies hadn't been fully zipped up.

'Busy with another lady guest?'

'Don't look at me like that. You were feeling frisky enough when I came to your room earlier this afternoon. I don't believe you got that way on your own. Anyway,' he grinned, 'it's not as if I've worn myself out.'

Heather wondered why she didn't feel as affronted as she'd tried to sound. Up until this weekend she'd been . . . romantic. Now the certainty that he'd just been with another woman put an edge on her appetite.

'I repeat my question,' he said. 'How d'you feel about leather?'

'I could be persuaded about its possibilities.'

Liam smiled and ran his tongue over his lips.

'My room's nearest,' he said, jerking his thumb towards the maze of small bedrooms in the converted stable block where the domestic staff stayed overnight when necessary. 'I share with another fella and I'm not sure what time he gets off duty.'

Heather stood up straighter, pulled back her shoulders and pushed her high breasts out towards him.

'If he shows up we'll let him watch. Come on.'

She followed Liam up a narrow, dog-legged staircase to a room barely big enough for two single beds and a copious amount of luggage. It wasn't the most sophisticated of settings, but Heather wasn't feeling particularly upmarket.

One holdall was unzipped. She reached in and found a large number of what could only be described as leather bandages: long, thick, black and made of very soft leather.

'You use these for tying women up?' she asked.
'Can do.'
'Tie me up.'
'You realise what you're asking?'
'Yes. Tie me up and do the dirtiest things you can imagine.'
'I can imagine a lot.' Liam grinned. 'You asked for it.'

He grabbed the neckline of her summer dress and ripped it off without bothering to undo the buttons. The fabric tore. Heather was glad. It was a little girl dress and she didn't want it any more. He pulled off her bra and panties just as roughly and, seizing her breasts, used them to push her down on to the bed, where he bound her wrists and ankles to the four corners with the leather straps.

Liam knelt above her and took out his cock. It was almost hard. She wondered who he'd already fucked with it that evening and, if this hard on was any indication, how many times he could go on to do it again. She parted her lips, more than willing to suck him off in this submissive position. But Liam shook his head and began to masturbate slowly.

Heather shivered with excitement. He was going to come all over her! It was going to be a carbon copy of what Robin had done to that marketing woman in the woods earlier that day. Robin . . . she closed her eyes and imagined him furiously wanking his beautiful pierced cock above her. She convinced herself it really was him as Liam's spunk fell in warm, thick spurts all over her face and breasts.

Then he untied her – but not for long. He turned her over and tied her face down again on the bed. She could just about turn her head to the side to see. And what she saw was Liam taking a cat-o'-nine-tails with long, knotted thongs, out of the bag.

'Poke your ass in the air,' he told her. 'I've given you enough slack.'

Obediently Heather did. She held her breath to listen for the click of the door and Liam's room mate returning. She almost hoped he would.

Liam brought the whip down firmly on her upthrust ass. It wasn't painful. It was . . . extreme. Of course – she'd heard Robin say that when describing the act of piercing his beautiful cock. Now she understood.

Liam flicked her ass again and again. Every time the cat fell she got more used to the feeling. After a few more moments she was loving it. The stinging sensation sent waves of pleasure over her glowing buttocks and warm ripples deep into her quim. Heather moaned. It was, she decided, the ideal prelude to penetration. And, despite the way Alex had fucked her almost raw that morning, she was longing to be penetrated again.

Liam put down the cat-o'-nine-tails. She saw him draw his thick motorcycle gauntlet on to his right hand. He stroked her buzzing labia for a moment, then slipped between them and enthusiastically finger fucked her.

Heather writhed with delight and clenched her vaginal muscles hard on his finger. In the heavy leather gauntlet it was as thick as a slimline cock. No one had finger fucked her for years. She'd forgotten the delicious possibilities.

A second leather-clad finger began working on her clitoris. This was absolute heaven. Her hard bud was being rubbed in just the right way but her quim wasn't going hungry. Heather moaned loudly as a particularly strong orgasm snaked up and possessed the centre of her body.

At the moment she came, Liam buried his head between her buttocks, kissed her asshole and flicked the tight, closed rosebud with his tongue.

'One day,' she heard him murmur. 'Soon . . .'

He untied her wrists and they relaxed for a while together, pressed close on the narrow single bed.

'Come on the road with me,' he whispered, 'and I could show you plenty more.'

It was tempting. The rarefied world of high-class ballet was losing its appeal right now. Nick would be furious. Heather giggled. It would be like running away to join the circus. For a while.

'Where are you going?' she asked.

'I've got to get to another job in Cornwall. Have to leave tomorrow evening, in fact, before this shebang folds up. The boss stretched his resources pretty thin to cater for this weekend.'

'The boss? You mean my brother?'

'No.' Liam shook his head. 'Nick Treganza isn't in charge.'

'I said lie down,' Robin repeated.

This time Lisette obeyed him.

She heard the rustle of last year's leaves as he knelt down behind her and began to undo her dress at the back. Then he reached round, pushed down the low neckline and eased out her heavy breasts. He placed them carefully over the white stone nipples of the image on the ground.

Lisette gasped. It was cold. The sensation was not unlike that of having her breasts cupped in old-fashioned champagne glasses filled with crushed ice. Yes, she knew that feeling. At least one lover had done it to her in the past.

'Stretch out on the giant,' she heard Robin say, as the intense, cold power flowed through her. 'Imagine his cock is inside you.'

She did. And it was easy to imagine. Such was the presence of the huge, pale phallus beneath her. It filled her, even stretched her. It seemed so very real.

Robin pushed her heavy brocade skirt up around the small of her back. Then she heard him chuckle – with approval presumably as she wasn't wearing any briefs.

She felt something trickle down the cleft of her ass. It was cold, like massage oil that hadn't been warmed. And there was a wave of the indefinable scent that seemed to have been following her all weekend. She knew her asshole was puckering in response to the trickling oil. A dead giveaway.

'I know more things than you realise,' he said. 'And now I think I know where your preferences lie.'

She felt Robin's fingers in her cleft, rubbing up and down her perineum, warming up the slippery lotion. She felt him add more, which he rimmed round and round her asshole. She heard the sound of a chunky metal zip being undone. She lifted her hips a little. She knew what was coming next.

Robin buggered her with no further preliminaries. She didn't need any. The thought of being penetrated by two stiff cocks at once was driving everything from her head. The giant's cock beneath her seemed very real – she was sure she could even feel it thrusting. The thin, stretched muscle between her ass and her quim was buzzing. She felt as if there was an explosion in her lower body as they came. And whether 'they' was two or three of them she found impossible to say.

Robin withdrew. Lisette rolled over, lazily, to look at him. She saw the thick silver ring in his detumescing cock. But unlike most women she didn't give him the satisfaction of gasping in surprise. Lisette wasn't easily shocked. No, for once she was more interested in the man's face.

'You bastard,' she finally said.

'Bastard? Is that any way to talk to a man who fixed it so you won that beautiful necklace and then gave you what I'd like to think was a pretty good fuck?'

'It's not that. But I do get to see run-of-the-mill invoices Nick wouldn't lower himself to bother with. I've just worked it out. Doesn't he know you're here?'

'What do you think? It's pretty sweet to have just buggered Nick's wife. Even sweeter if she knows who I am.'

'Don't flatter yourself. You're not the only one with a trick up your sleeve. Can you keep a secret?'

'I keep lots of secrets.'

Chapter Nine

HEATHER SAT ALMOST alone in the breakfast room whose wide open French windows looked over the lake. A slight breeze reached her. She held her second cup of coffee in two hands and watched the world over its wide rim. Even the rich Kenyan blend couldn't quite mask the sweet muskiness of sex clinging to her long fingers.

She hadn't stayed long in Liam's bed. Not that she'd been afraid of his room mate walking in and finding them. She'd been hoping he would. But the bed was narrow. She needed her sleep. She'd gone back to her own room and slept right through her travel alarm.

Liam wasn't serving at breakfast. Rebelliously, Heather had ordered the full English cooked, smiling as she imagined the expression on her dance teacher's face. She crushed the whole, succulent mushrooms between her tongue and the roof of her mouth, relishing their oiliness. She'd had enough of denial, of keeping her weight spare in the hope of playing the dying swan. What sort of life was that? When she danced again it would be dances of a very different kind.

One thought did cross her mind. Why were there so few people about? Few party guests. Few staff, for that matter. Sure it was twenty-to-ten but after the treasure hunt and goodness knew what else last night, they couldn't all have been up bright and early and had breakfast already. Could they? The hotel seemed quiet as if the old Hall was holding its breath. For something.

In the absence of any other diversions Heather decided on self-indulgence. The dance school didn't approve of sunbathing. They liked their English roses pale and interesting. Half an hour later Heather was down on the sloping lawns by the lake, with a bottle of sunblock and wearing only the briefest pair of tanga bikini bottoms and a sarong. She soon laid the sarong down on the grass.

Still no one was about. Heather did feel pleased with herself, though – sunbathing topless out here, far from the nearest cover. She felt a new sense of wantonness creep across her as she massaged the creamy sunblock into her breasts. She enjoyed their hard texture, the resistance they gave against her palms. When she'd finished she stretched her arms languorously above her head and opened herself to the sun's caress – a sensual, omnipresent lover.

Next thing Heather knew a shadow was falling over her and she hadn't noticed anyone approach. She sat up and shaded her eyes.

'You need some more sunblock,' Robin said, squatting down to her level. Looking at her breasts, he continued, 'They don't look as if they're used to much exposure. Want some help rubbing it in?'

Heather leaned back, taking her weight on her elbows, and tilted her chest towards him. This is what she'd been waiting for. Robin was about to touch her sexually.

'Help yourself. The bottle's just down there.'

Robin poured a generous creamy handful into his palm. Then he smeared it across her chest and began to massage it in. His fingers worked on her, slow and masterful. She relaxed and let them glide across her slippery white breasts.

This was extravagance. Robin and Liam – in her mind there wasn't a conflict. It was like being offered an expensive box of Belgian chocolates: one time you'd take a rum truffle, another time a praline. It didn't mean you liked one more than the other. They were both there for the choosing. To gratify an appetite. And Heather was going to explore her appetites more. She imagined her body filling out under the satisfaction, finding its natural, womanly form. Another sort of grace: voluptuous, sensual. Like – say – Eleni's.

When Robin had diligently rubbed every last trace of lotion into her breasts he bent to circle first one nipple then the other with his tongue. Heather gasped as his short beard touched the ultra sensitive skin round her areolae. It was everything she'd imagined it to be. The springy hairs caressed her like a lover's tiny thousand fingertips, but more mobile, more exploratory than anything she'd experienced before. The touch of a hand, or even a tongue, now seemed gross and insensitive by comparison. Her skin was dancing with sensation. She wanted more. It was time, she told herself. It was finally time to discover the mysteries of his pierced cock.

Heather shifted her weight on to one arm and reached for his flies. Robin caught her hand in mid air.

'All in good time,' he said. 'Would you like to join the real party now?'

'The real party?' Heather frowned. No, she hadn't just been paranoid. There really was something going on that no one had told her about. 'Is that where everyone's disappeared to?'

Robin stood up and held out his hand towards her. 'Come on.'

Heather retrieved her sarong, wrapped it round herself and followed him towards the woods.

Jenna writhed against the chains that bound her wrists but nothing gave. She hadn't really expected it to. The tent pole Robin and Liam had tethered her to was as sturdy as ever. It was torture, though – a man on each side of her, each a total stranger, each with his hands tied behind his back.

The men were tonguing her dark, pouting nipples through the slits that readily opened in what Robin had called her 'slave dress'. The nipple stimulation was driving her crazy with randiness but, tied up like that, neither she nor the men could do anything about it. She must have been on the verge of coming for more than an hour.

Robin and the young Irish waiter had brought her here the previous night, after their adventures deep in the woods. Here, to the largest of the medieval marquees in the clearing of the lion-masked giant.

'Consider yourself still well and truly kidnapped,' Robin had told her. 'Now you're our slave. And a slave's got to wear . . . something appropriate.'

Then he'd produced the dress. Jenna had never

seen anything like it before. It was made entirely of fine, silvery chains, arranged so they hung down from the neckline. As he slipped it over her head she saw its purpose.

The chains fell aside naturally over her prominent breasts to expose them, frame them, draw attention to them even more than if she'd been completely naked. And if she lay down – as she was doing now – the weight of the chain skirt settled uncompromisingly between her thighs, like the heel of a hand pressing down on her mons. A diffuse stimulation, not enough to make her come but sure as hell enough so that by now she would have done anything, agreed to anything, just to get sexual release.

Robin and Liam had stepped back, then, as if to admire their work. Outside in the clearing, many torches had been blazing. The light had flickered through gaps in the canvas and its reflections licked her chains.

'Yes,' Robin had murmured to Liam at last. 'She looks suitably subservient, don't you think? Covered and at the same time uncovered. Exquisitely available.'

'Why are you doing this to me?' Jenna demanded.

Robin winked. 'Don't pretend you're not enjoying it. Ah.' He cocked his head as if he'd heard a sound outside. 'Seems like the expected company has arrived.' He peered through one of the canvas slits. 'I'll just give her a moment . . .'

Soon afterwards he put his finger to his lips conspiratorially and slipped out. Liam shackled Jenna's handcuffs to a post and then left through another flap. Some time later – after what sounded like gasps and grunts of lovemaking – Jenna heard voices. She couldn't pick out what they were saying but was fairly certain they were Robin's and Lisette's.

They left her alone till early morning. Liam brought her breakfast and then her second course: the two strangers who were lying naked and bound beside her now and who were demonstrably enjoying her breasts.

And she was enjoying the fervent ministrations of their tongues. To have both breasts at once warmly sucked, flicked, circled by a mobile tongue was heaven. Too often this delight would have been over quickly – the man too eager to get his swollen prick somewhere warm and moist and to come. But these men – shackled as much as she was – were incapable of doing anything but rolling their erections against her thighs. And this was sweet, too. Such an obvious sign of how much her body turned them on.

The tent flap opened. Robin came in. He stood for a moment, arms folded across his chest, watching Jenna's constrained pleasuring with obvious satisfaction. His leather trousers moulded to his own erection.

She still couldn't decide whether she was furious with him for playing these games or simply glad he was there. Having him watching her while the two men stimulated her breasts turned her on even more. Perhaps, at long last, she was going to feel that kinky pierced cock enter her.

But Robin made no move to unzip his flies. Instead he knelt down between her parted thighs, brushed aside the delicate chains that covered her sex and began to tongue her slowly.

She gasped at his technique. A lazy but thorough flick up and down the full length of her labia. As if he was, quite literally, lapping up her plentiful juice. He was taking his time. He seemed to be genuinely enjoying what he was doing.

At last he wriggled the tip of his tongue between her slick, dark lips. He snaked it into her as far as it would go. Robin had a long tongue. She imagined it going into her as deep as any cock.

For several minutes he rolled and writhed it against the firm, muscular walls of her sex. She loved that feeling. No cock was so prehensile. It was unique.

Then he withdrew his tongue and flicked it slowly up and down her clitoris – at last. All morning she'd been frantic to be touched there. Three men, three tongues, each worshipping a separate tight, erectile bud of her desire. The whole centre of Jenna's body dissolved into a lazy, honeyed orgasm.

When she opened her eyes again she wasn't sure how much time had passed. She and Robin were alone in the tent. He'd obviously released the other two men to go and find their satisfaction elsewhere. Then Robin took a small silvery key from a hidden pocket in his leather jerkin, reached past her and unlocked the handcuffs around her wrists.

Jenna sat up, rubbing furiously at her biceps and deltoids. She must have been restrained like that for hours. She couldn't decide which feeling should be uppermost, and battled between relief at being free and the exciting possibility that she and Robin were finally . . .

She reached for him. He didn't move away. She cupped his leather-clad groin. It was hard, bursting with promise. Through the tight black trousers that moulded to him like a living thing she could almost feel the tension in his balls. She nestled her face against him. Lost her senses in the heady, overpowering, animal smell of leather.

Jenna traced the line of his hard, proud cock with her middle finger. She found the even harder, unyielding outline of the ring. She fancied his erection shifted subtly in response to her touch. But when she reached to grasp the chunky brass zip, to undo his flies and take his cock head in her mouth, Robin grasped her hand.

'Patience,' he said. 'This one's promised.'

'You bastard,' she spat out. 'You've done just about everything except fuck me.'

Robin smiled. It was that maddening smile which told her yet again, There are so many things you don't understand. And I'm not going to let you – yet.

'Everything in its proper order,' he said and left the tent.

Nick woke up alone. And in those few moments when the body adjusts to where it is waking up in an unfamiliar room the impression came – before anything else – that something was wrong. Where was Lisette? Come to that, where the hell was everyone else? When he'd got back to the Hall last night only a few bored stragglers seemed to have returned from the treasure hunt. There'd been dissatisfaction in the air.

This wasn't how it was meant to be. The weekend wasn't following its scripted plan. Something had gone wrong. Nick didn't pay people for things to go wrong. Waking up alone on the very day of his thirtieth birthday he suddenly felt again like the abandoned boy no one wanted to know at school.

He couldn't face company. He wasn't in the mood

to go downstairs and play mine host at breakfast to a sullen, decimated crowd. So he rang room service and ordered the continental option to be sent up.

For a while he forgot about being irritated. The coffee was a smooth, dark roast. A warm and caffeine-laden slap in the face to bring him round. And the fresh-baked buttery croissants with their tiny dabs of melted plain chocolate lurking like a surprise. As he chewed he thought wryly that Lisette would have liked this. Such a breakfast would have put her in a co-operative mood. It usually did. Then his jaw tightened again. Where had his wife got to?

Nick threw on a robe and went to the window. She'd come down in her own yellow sports car, hadn't she? It was still there. So she was here somewhere. And, judging by the numbers of BMWs, Discoveries and Rovers parked on the gravel, so was everyone else. But they were keeping very quiet about it.

His gaze panned over the hotel grounds. And stopped. There was a couple by the lake, but they were too far away for him to tell who they were.

He narrowed his eyes. The woman was lying on her back on the grass. Was she wearing anything at all? Maybe. Maybe just the tiniest pair of bikini briefs. And the man was pouring some sun cream into his hand – rubbing it into her breasts. Nick's cock tightened automatically at the thought.

He had to come. It was a compulsion. He had to come and come again. He lay back on the bed, undid the belt on his robe and lovingly began to handle his cock.

It responded to his touch. He was torn between pride in its potency and humiliation that he should have to do this for himself. It was his weekend. Jenna,

Lisette, Eleni – any one of those women should have been available to satisfy him. But – Nick closed his eyes – wanking really did feel so good.

There was a knock at the door.

Nick tensed. His hand froze on his cock. Interrupted in such delicious self indulgence, he was tempted to wait till whoever it was gave up and went away. But . . . Lisette wouldn't have knocked. It might be Jenna. Or Eleni.

Another knock.

'Come in,' he called, twitching his robe back over his detumescing cock.

One of the redhead waitresses walked in. 'I told you one or other of us would be round sometime over the weekend to "collect".'

Today she was back in a more conventional waitress's uniform. A tight black skirt coming half way down her thighs. Black fishnets – he assumed they must be stockings. A little white blouse that hugged her curves and whose material was thin enough to show the tantalising outline of a lacy white bra. But it showed no more than that. Fully clothed, Nick still couldn't tell the twins apart. And she seemed to know that, and was enjoying seeing him wonder.

'What do you want?' he asked, dry-mouthed, 'if you don't want cash? Are you permanent staff? After a management position? I'll see what I can—'

She laughed. But worse than that, she laughed at him. Nick couldn't cope with that.

'You've got us all wrong,' she said. 'Actually we're going to do you a favour.'

'What?'

'We're going to help you get over your sexual hang-ups.'

'Sexual hang-ups? Me? I haven't got any.'
'That's not what I've heard.'

She reached for a black carry-all by the door. He hadn't noticed her bring it in. He'd been too busy watching her – the sexy, confident way she moved. She unzipped the bag and began to take things out.

When she straightened up there were several lengths of soft, dark leather in her hands. Nick didn't doubt their purpose. His pulse began to beat a little faster and, with the blood pumping round his body, he felt life returning to his hidden cock. No woman had ever tied him up. He'd never permitted it. It spoke of humiliation: meant loss of control. But now ... he began to feel the time was ripe for a little experimentation.

So Nick co-operated fully as she wrapped the soft, thick leather straps round his wrists and ankles. He didn't protest as she tied him to the four corners of the bed, pinning his limbs wide as she did so. When she was sure he was tied securely she opened his robe. With his legs spread Nick's cock and balls felt very, very vulnerable.

'I see,' she murmured, looking with approval at his erection, 'you're obviously beginning to enjoy things already.'

Nick relaxed and grinned back at her. He had a fair idea what was coming next. She wanted to be the boss? Well, he'd play along. She'd strip off real slow while he was helpless to do anything but watch her. She'd mount him, teasing him with her body, dangling those luscious breasts (pierced or unpierced? He was desperate to know) just out of reach of his gaping mouth. It would be delicious torture. She'd make him plead a bit. Okay, he'd go along. Then at last she'd take pity on him, go down and engulf his stiff prick in her lipsticked mouth and suck him till he climaxed quickly and explosively and she'd swallow his come.

The girl stepped back from the bed. It looked like Nick's guess was right. She'd begun undoing the buttons, one by one, on that tight little white blouse. She let it fall to the floor. The stiff lace bra beneath was thrusting her breasts upwards – much to Nick's delight. His cock twitched. And there, just where the plump, freckled flesh was beginning to slip out of its lacy prison, was the dark beginnings of a tattoo. Nick shivered a little – fascinated now more than repelled. In the past he'd never really approved of tattooed women. But if this was therapy to get over it, it sure as hell was fun.

She unhooked her bra and jiggled her big breasts for him – very, very aware of how much it was turning him on. Nick stared at her pierced nipples. They looked so pouting, so big, so permanently ready to be tongued. Perhaps that was the idea. Perhaps they were.

She unzipped her little black skirt and a wriggle of her hips sent it slithering to the carpet. And yes, she was wearing stockings beneath. The black suspenders cut across her soft, pale thighs. She stepped out of her black satin panties and, Nick noted with pleasure, seemed to have no intention to remove the rest. Fine. He loved being teased by a woman wearing stockings, suspenders and leather high heels.

He waited for her to come and rub her body over him. But then she began to deviate from Nick's mental script.

She reached into the carry-all and pulled out something else. When Nick realised what it was an iciness began in his chest and spread through his body. He was terrified. Not only of the thing itself but of losing his erection while the sexy redhead watched.

'I told you,' she murmured, watching his reaction, 'I was going to help you with phobias like that.'

She lifted the snake. It wreathed itself round her, hungry for warmth. One muscular coil looped between her breasts. Nick stared. It was horrifying – and compelling.

And it reminded him of something. Pictures he'd seen of dangerous, alluring women. Old sepia prints of *fin de siècle* exotic dancers. In his early days with Lisette she'd made him traipse round galleries and exhibitions of just such photographs. Nick had pretended an interest he didn't really share, as it had been imperative to convince Lisette he was the one.

He remembered one gallery in particular. And one photo of a long-dead Parisian fan dancer who'd used a snake as part of her act. Her stage name had been Lilith. Damn. He'd stood, swallowed hard, and forced himself to look at the sepia photograph. He couldn't afford to let Lisette see that chink in his armour – and to this day he never had.

But no, he hadn't lost his erection. Because fear, revulsion and desire were binding him tightly like a three-strand rope. The redhead was pleasuring herself. He couldn't take his eyes off her.

She cupped her heavy breasts in her own hands, lifting them and rolling their prominent, pierced nipples between thumb and forefinger. She looked for all the world as if she was doing this solely for her own satisfaction. Maybe she was. Nick, trussed up on the bed, was quite incidental. The thought drove him crazy.

Now she was gliding her hands slowly down her body. Her fingertips rippled – with apparently equal enjoyment – over her own curves and those of the snake.

'What have you got against them?' she asked, her eyes closed.

'I had a run-in with one once,' Nick replied – aware that it wasn't exactly an answer.

'Don't tell me – you were brought up somewhere exotic. India? South Africa?'

'Basingstoke actually.'

'So was it poisonous? Escaped from a zoo?'

'I don't know. And no, not really . . .'

He trailed off because she didn't seem to be listening. Her fingers had come to rest between her thighs. She raked them once or twice through her glossy auburn bush. Then she tilted back her head and parted her labia.

She began to masturbate. From the look on her face – eyes still closed, lips parted – there was no play acting about her pleasure. She was taunting him. Every sinuous buck and writhe of her desirable body said, Look, I can satisfy myself. You are unnecessary to me. Nick, with his hard cock straining for her, could hardly have been more insulted.

His balls were aching with the orgasm her arrival had denied him. He longed to have his hands free to wank himself again. He struggled against the leather bonds but they weren't for show. They were genuinely inescapable. Perhaps that was her game. She wanted to hear him plead. To hear him grovel for the release her mouth or her hands or her warm, tight pussy could give. Well okay. She'd won. Nick licked his lips and parted them ready to beg.

There was another knock at the door.

It was staccato this time – a strange rhythm like a pre-arranged code. The redhead withdrew her middle finger slowly from her quim. It was slick and glistening with her own ready-flowing juice.

'Come in, Sis,' she said. 'It's open.'

Her twin walked in. She too was dressed in a formal waitress's uniform, the only difference being that her black stockings were sheer, not fishnet. They made a hoarse whisper, thigh swishing against thigh, as she walked over to Nick on the bed.

'He seems ready,' she said, looking at the straining erection and, Nick imagined, the pleading in his eyes. 'Let's go for it.'

She undressed quickly in a business-like way. But she too left her stockings and high heels on. Meanwhile her twin untangled herself from the snake and began undoing Nick's leather trusses. He was free only for a moment, though. They tied his wrists behind his back.

Nick found himself upright beside the bed with his erection sticking straight out in front of him. He was in the infuriating position of being confronted by two statuesque pairs of breasts but unable to fondle them.

The newcomer sat down on the high-backed dressing table chair. The other twin forced Nick to bend down over her sister's lap. The seated twin caught his stiff prick between her whispering nylon-clad thighs. Nick rolled his hips experimentally to see how much stimulation he could get. Quite a lot. He was sure he was close to ejaculation.

Then he heard a sound as if someone was rummaging through the carry-all again. He craned his head to see the pierced twin coming back with a small black leather riding crop.

'Lie still,' she barked. 'And you don't come until we give you permission to.'

She brought the crop down smartly on his ass. The little leather flap at the end gave a sudden cracking sound he hadn't been expecting. This, more than the physical sensation, made him jump.

'I said, "Lie still"!' she repeated. 'I know your cock is hard. I know you want to shoot your load and have done with it. But we haven't finished with you. You're to lie still. No rubbing yourself off between my sister's thighs.'

Nick tried his best to comply. He was almost breathless. She brought the crop down again – one, two, three – in quick succession. He'd never been so much as smacked as a child. Of course, his trendy liberal father hadn't agreed with it. Now, as three more blows rained down on his bare buttocks, he realised it wasn't actually hurting him. It was extreme. But it wasn't pain. Every new blow that fell brought a fresh glowing feeling to his upturned ass. Every time the crop smacked down on his flesh it sent a jolt through him – but an agreeable jolt that ended with a tickle of pleasure just at the deep-seated, hidden root of his cock.

'Look at his face,' his dominatrix commented. 'Now he's got used to it he's enjoying it. He's just as much of a tart as we thought. Let's see now . . . Let's see what other kinky games he might like.'

She stopped. Nick was almost in tears at the thought. He wanted to beg her to continue. That sort of unexpected sexual pleasure was addictive. He knew he had to be tied up and spanked again soon.

But . . . how could he ask Jenna or Eleni? And Lisette didn't even bear thinking about. All those women had been seduced by his ultra male dominance. Perhaps he needed to go in search of a new type of woman altogether.

He raised his head to see what the sisters were doing now. One twin was standing at the dressing table. She'd found a bottle of Lisette's moisturising lotion – one of many. She was carefully anointing the handle of the riding crop with it. Nick had a fair idea of what was going to happen next. He was powerless to stop it.

She advanced, holding the slick end of the riding crop towards him. Her sister grasped the cheeks of Nick's ass and stretched them wide. He felt the knobbly end of the handle rim his asshole – once, twice, three times. Then one or other of the women plunged it into him. It touched a deeply hidden, secret, receptive seat of sexual pleasure and he cried out loud with unexpected joy.

The twin beneath him closed her thighs against his prick. She took the crop and began to pleasure him slowly but thoroughly with the handle. Each stroke hit that perfect trigger spot of pleasure. He only wished he'd discovered this years ago.

The other twin – the pierced one – reached down beneath her sister's stockinged thighs and began to fondle the very tip of his cock. But it wasn't necessary. He was already at the point of no return.

Nick's stiff prick ejaculated violently straight down towards the carpet. He was coming and coming – it felt like a dam had been breached.

What on earth would the hotel cleaners say?

He felt utterly humiliated. If Lisette, Jenna, or

anyone else who worked with him found out about this how could he ever bear the shame?

And he wanted to do it again as soon as humanly possible.

Chapter Ten

HEATHER WASN'T SURPRISED where she and Robin ended up. The clearing with the lion-faced giant. Everything came back to there.

He'd squeezed her upper arm lightly before he left. 'I've got things to organise. I'll see you in a little while. Why don't you wait in that tent?'

He'd pointed out a dusky purple tent. It was the sort of thing you might have found in the desert. A place for a Bedouin leader to seduce his virgin bride. But here it was in the middle of a very English oakwood. Heather felt drawn to it. She skirted the lion-man image on the way. There was a power about it, even in dappled daylight with people going in and out of tents and lazing in the spaces between them.

The purple one was quiet, though. As if waiting for someone. Heather lifted the tent flap and went in.

If she'd ever had any preconceptions about tents – girl guides, sleeping bags, crushed grass, airlessness – they fell around her feet.

This was high-vaulted, roomy and airy. The ground was covered with rugs and bright satin scatter cushions. The Bedouin warlord seducing his doe-like bride with sybaritic luxury came back to the forefront of her daydreams. There was an oil-burner in the middle of the tent. Little wisps of smoke curled up from it and stroked the still air lazily, lovingly. The scent from it was all mossiness and muskiness. Again.

Curled cat-like on a heap of cushions in the far corner was Eleni.

She'd abandoned her guise as seductress of the Nile. Possibly, Heather thought, she'd had it stripped off her once too often that weekend and couldn't be bothered putting it on again. But the acid in that thought evaporated all too soon. Eleni wasn't her rival.

The older woman rose to greet her. She was wearing a sky blue sarong now – not unlike Heather's own. But her figure filled it out. A gap opened in the fabric as she walked, from just below her left breast all the way down the front of her thigh. Heather was sure she was naked underneath.

'Welcome,' Eleni said, taking the girl's hands in hers and kissing her on the cheek. 'I'd been hoping you'd show up.'

'Hoping?'

'Yes.' Eleni kept hold of one hand and guided Heather back down on to the yielding silky cushions. 'You've got a story to tell, I'm sure. That "unfinished business" last night? I expect you finished it. That sparkle in your eyes tells me so.'

That first night in the ballroom Heather had disliked Eleni instantly. She'd been everything Heather couldn't be – wanton, voluptuous, sure of her own sexual magnetism. Heather hated women like that. Women who cast their eyes sideways at any man they wanted and he'd come running.

It wasn't like that any more. Heather was changing, learning. Why – she and Eleni could even be friends.

She settled herself into the rich fabric beside Eleni and prepared to give as good as she got.

'Fair's fair. I take it you went off with Morgan? Give me the goss.'

Like a sultry Scheherazade Eleni propped herself up on one elbow and began to tell her story. The gap in her sarong closed fully over her brown skin as she did so. Heather felt a twinge of disappointment at this. And then confusion that she did so.

'I found him just after I left you last night,' Eleni began. 'He made a big thing about wanting to go off on the treasure hunt. But I knew he didn't mean it. Not when he was looking at me like that. He couldn't take his eyes off these.' She cupped her voluptuous breasts and lifted them. Under the thin sarong material Heather could see Eleni's nipples were peaking. She felt a shiver of jealousy that went straight to her clitoris. But it wasn't just jealousy. She was curious too.

'I'd imagine a lot of men find it difficult to keep their eyes off your . . . breasts,' she said hesitantly.

'You bet,' Eleni replied, continuing to glide her palms over the flimsy sky blue fabric. 'Where was I? Yes. Morgan. He had charge of the first set of clues. He liked that. Being in charge. I didn't argue about which way we went – even though after a while I knew damn well we weren't finding any more clues.

'We ended up back at the hotel. In the health suite. Did you know there was a health suite? No, me neither. We've all been indulging ourselves, not trying to get fit. I said, "What are we doing here?" and he just said, "Get your top off. You've been driving me nuts."

'So I unwound all that ridiculous Cleopatra head-dress and peeled off that skimpy little push-up metallic bra. And he just stands there for ages staring at my chest and licking his lips as if he's awe-struck. So I say, "Hey, I know what men think of beauties like these. I'm proud to have them, to tell you the truth. What do you want to do? Feel them? Suck them? Get your cock out and rub it up and down till you come in my face?"'

Eleni was getting herself turned on, Heather could tell. She was rolling and squeezing her own breasts and the tone of her voice had gone ragged. Heather longed to touch Eleni too. Longed to reach over, feel that soft, voluptuous body and share its rising sexual excitement. But she couldn't. Eleni was a mere few inches away across the soft silk cushions. But still Heather couldn't bring herself to touch her.

Eleni continued, 'But he said, "Get on that pec deck. Pump some iron, woman. I want to see you work out. Make 'em jiggle and bounce." So I did. I got on the machine and he set the weight real high and I heaved my arms together. I guess it's like one of those "bust developer" things some school girls use. Never needed to. I've always been big. But Morgan comes and stands in front of me while I'm pressing my elbows – in and out, in and out. I can feel my breasts jiggling and jumping like mad with each press. I mean, there's nothing to hold the big guys back – I'm stark naked above the waist. And I know his eyes are clamped on that jiggle. He's really getting off on it. The bulge in the front of those tight black leather trousers – why, it's huge!

'And finally I give in. I don't pump iron, kiddo. My muscles are killing me. There's sweat running all down my cleavage. Morgan comes over to me. He unzips his flies. His cock must have been agony in there! And then he rubs it up and down a bit between my breasts. They're so slippery with sweat. It glides nice and smooth and easy.

'Then he puts it to my lips. It's salty and delicious by now. So I can't resist sucking it. I tell myself I'll just suck it for a little bit. Just to show I like it. And I do, I do. I'm so horny by now. I want it in me. I don't want it to end yet. But he must have been closer than I thought. There I am, sat in this machine looking like I'm a prisoner – though I'm not – and just the right height to suck cock. And while I'm doing it he grasps my tits and squeezes them and then he comes like champagne going pop in my mouth and I swallow it all down.'

Eleni opened her eyes and licked her lips at the memory. 'I just love sucking cock. I love the feel of it between my lips. The responsiveness. Ahh ... But then, you know what the bastard does? While I'm randy as hell and aching for him to get a hard on again and give it to me long and rough he says, "Eleni, the treasure hunt must be over by now. I've got an appointment to meet Robin in the woods. Coming?" And by that point I really wish I was. So I follow him, my clitoris thrumming like crazy and my head's going wild with what Morgan'll do to me when we've got wherever we're going. And when we do – here – I'm left alone in this tent. Heather' – one hand left her breast, reached over and touched the girl's arm – 'I haven't had a lover all night.'

Heather froze. Was Eleni trying to seduce her? She'd thought the woman a total man-eater. Was it possible? Could she be all things at once? Confused, she tried to play for time.

'Sorry to hear you went without. I didn't. With

Liam – that gorgeous young Irish waiter. Want to hear about it?'

Eleni nodded. But as she did so her warm body seemed to shift a few inches closer to Heather's until they were almost touching.

Heather licked her lips and hesitated, aware her storytelling skills weren't up to Eleni's. She'd never done this before. Never shared really intimate details beyond "Yeah, we did it". Where was she supposed to start?

'He's into leather,' she began. 'I'd never thought about it before. The way it moulds against your skin. The scent of it. You breathe it in deep like it's tickling your nostrils and your lungs all the way down. A little spicy. Animal. There's nothing like it.

'He had some stuff. Bands. Like he'd done this all before. He tied me up with them. I couldn't move – but it was gentle. He tied me up and finger-fucked me from behind.'

Eleni shifted again. Now her big, soft, silk-bound breasts were pressing against Heather's. As their nipples touched – barely separated by the thin fabric both women wore – Heather felt an illicit thrill shiver through her. No doubt about it. She was on the point of being seduced by another woman. And she was in no mood to fight it.

'That isn't all,' she continued, becoming very aware of Eleni's ticklish breath on her neck. 'The door wasn't locked. Liam's room mate could have come in at any time. Seen me trussed up in black leather with my ass in the air.'

Eleni's lips began to peck softly at Heather's neck. Not quite a bite. Not quite a kiss. It was sensual yet just on the edge of danger.

'What if he had? Were you afraid?'

'No. Normally I would be but not by then. I was just so crazy with this whole new thing. Part of me was hoping he would walk in. The risk felt sexy.'

'If he had would you have liked him to watch?'

'Depends. If I'd fancied him too . . .'

'You'd have liked him to join in?'

'I was getting greedy by then. Feeling dizzy and heady from doing something I'd never done. Yeah – I'd have loved him to join in.'

Heather felt Eleni's hand close on her tight, high breast. No woman had ever touched her there. Eleni's long fingers seemed expert. Heather's nipples were already drawing into hard pert nubs as she remembered what she'd done last night. And what she might have done. Eleni teased them very lightly, just brushing a thumb pad round and round, over and over. Subtler than a man's touch, more knowing, more controlled. Both felt good.

'I hope you get to try it,' Eleni whispered. 'Threesomes are fantastic – either way. You can have it, Heather. Here. This weekend. You can have it all.'

She kissed Heather on the mouth – fully, deeply, uncompromisingly. Her lips were fuller than a man's, her cheeks free from the stubble Heather had come to expect. It felt natural, sisterly, sharing.

It was time to give something back. Heather pulled at the edge of Eleni's liquid silk, sky blue sarong. It parted easily.

She had never been so close to another woman's breasts – never had time to take in the scent, the softness, the feel of them. She took her time now.

Heather ran her tongue down Eleni's tanned cleavage, amazed at how firm was the valley that separated those two billowing hemispheres. She loved their softness. She could have spent all day kissing their slopes and curves, weighing their heaviness in each hand. She sucked each nipple, doing just what she'd like a man to do to her. Eleni's nipples were prominent. Edible. She flicked her tongue lightly, rapidly over the very tip.

Eleni gave a deep moan and writhed. She threw her legs round Heather's hips and kept her locked there, prisoner. Heather couldn't believe how much she was turning the other woman on. Here she was – a virgin as far as lesbian sex was concerned. But under her hands, lips and tongue Eleni was practically gasping with need. The power she had! Heather felt sexy and strong.

She lifted her face from Eleni's breasts. At the same time she reached down and touched her friend between her thighs. Eleni relaxed her leg-grip on Heather's hips. Heather glided her fingers into the other woman's soft bush. She found an entrance that was inviting and slick.

'What do you want me to do?'

'I was hoping to be the judge of that.'

Heather froze. The voice was not Eleni's.

She looked up. Robin was standing by the tent flap, watching them. He must have come in so quietly. She didn't know how long he'd been there. Eleni's muscles didn't so much as twitch. Either she was very cool or she'd been expecting this. Heather didn't know whether to be furious with her. She tried to feel angry. Tried to feel conned. But she couldn't. Later, maybe. For now she was too turned on. Desire came first. And besides, Robin . . .

Apart from his leather jerkin he was naked from the

waist up. She realised she'd never seen his naked chest before. The scattering of dark hair was inviting. She wanted to run her hands through it. And there was a single silver ring just below his left nipple, too. It didn't surprise her. She wanted to flick it, to see what effect it had on him. His black leather trousers clung to his slim hips. She wanted to see him drop them. She wanted another look at that fascinating pierced cock.

As if sensing this he began to unzip his flies. He was wearing nothing beneath. But he didn't completely drop his trousers. He only slipped them down enough to free his erection and hold it proudly in his hand.

'On second thoughts, don't mind me.' He grinned. 'You two looked like you were getting on just fine. Don't let me interrupt.'

Heather met Eleni's eyes. There was a calm, amused look there. One that reminded her, *It's okay. You can have it all.*

'What do you want me to do?' Heather said again out loud.

Eleni parted her legs further and relaxed back on to the cushions. 'Use your tongue on me, darling.'

'But I'm not sure . . .'

'You'll be fine. You'll know what to do.'

As Heather went down between Eleni's thighs she glanced up and saw the other woman begin to fondle her own big breasts. Eleni's dark pubic hair was springy against her face. She rubbed her nose in it. The sweet smell of sex – like her own but subtly different. Spicier, maybe. More exotic. Her friend's quim was slippery with excitement.

I did that, Heather thought. *I turned her on. Me – inexperienced as I am. I can take her all the way.*

She poked out her tongue as far as it would go. She

drew it backwards and forwards between Eleni's plump lips. She delved as far as she could, wriggling it into the other woman's welcoming sex. Eleni moaned in gratitude. Heather went back to the soft back and forth strokes but this time at the end of each stroke she gave the clitoris a little circle and a flick.

Eleni was rolling her hips. Heather knew this was an automatic reaction to an orgasm coming on. Part of her didn't want it to end so soon. She was enjoying the playfulness of tonguing another woman more than she would ever have thought possible. And Eleni's struggling made things difficult. Heather seized her friend's hip bones and pinned her to the cushions to keep her still.

Eleni gasped, as if amazed and aroused by this sudden dominance in someone so virgin with her own sex. Heather tongued her clitoris like crazy. Eleni cried out and strained against Heather's hold – but the dancer was stronger than she'd imagined. As Eleni gave a long drawn out moan and the mons beneath Heather's mouth began to pulse, Heather realised she'd made her first female lover come.

The thought made her hornier than ever.

The women looked up at Robin who, judging by the still-high erection cradled in his hand, had been enjoying the show. And then in a move that seemed previously choreographed, Eleni pulled Heather back to lie against her, reached round, hooked her hands over Heather's thighs and spread them wide.

This time it was Heather pinned in a body bondage. She knew, with the powerful, disciplined muscles in her thighs, she could undoubtedly break free from Eleni's grip if she wanted to. Eleni must suspect it too. But Heather didn't try.

Robin peeled off his tight leather trousers. He came to kneel between her open thighs. His pierced cock reared above her. It dominated everything.

Enter me, Heather silently prayed. Enter me. Please. This time. I've been waiting . . .

He bent over and began to tongue her nipples. Eleni let go her fierce grip on her thighs, reached round and began instead to cup and fondle Heather's breasts, raising them up to offer them to Robin's lips. Between them they stoked the fire in Heather's loins again, bringing her to desperation. When she was moaning, 'Please, please,' Robin dipped his hips and penetrated her.

For a moment she felt his cock-ring nudge her clitoris. Then the warmth and glide as he slid confidently into her, stretching her.

He rode her simply but every thrust was absolutely precise. Heather relaxed and submitted to the waves of unhurried pleasure building in her lower body. Robin placed his palms over Eleni's on her breasts. Their hands were never still. They roamed over her like four little animals squabbling over territory.

Heather felt so complete, so included as never before in her life. She vowed she must have three-way sex again as soon as possible. Always the outsider, the different one, the skinny one, the precious one who had to watch what she did and ate. Pressed between Robin and Eleni and their roving hands she let go. As she did so Robin's cock rode her into a slow-building, warm, blossoming orgasm.

He must have been holding back. As he felt her come he thrust deeper and cried and she knew he'd climaxed too. Still inside her he relaxed down. The three of them somehow had their arms around each other. It felt a very loving moment. Only after a long time, after three sets of heartbeats had quieted to almost normal did Heather realise the weight pressing on her.

'Hey,' she said, digging Robin in the ribs, 'give me some space, will you?'

He chuckled and rolled aside. But as he did so he caught her slim wrist and turned it over to look at her delicate gold watch.

'Didn't realise that was the time. Better arrange some lunch for the prisoner.'

'Prisoner! Who?'

'Three guesses.'

'Not . . . Nick?'

'Two guesses left.'

Jenna wasn't physically restrained. Robin had left her handcuffs unlocked this time. But there was a dark man-shaped shadow on the tent flap. It kept still. Standing to attention. She got the impression she wouldn't be allowed to leave.

She felt in limbo. What was going on? It was Sunday after all – classic 'in limbo' time. Neither working week nor party time. And was it really only Sunday? Less than forty-eight hours since she'd arrived at the Hall? Time was doing strange things.

Jenna could smell food. Something spicy. It was getting stronger. She hugged her belly. Somewhere along the way she'd lost her watch but she was sure it must be well past lunch time.

The tent flap opened. The first thing Jenna noticed was Alex, the American, with a tray of artfully arranged finger buffet food.

The second thing she noticed was that her shadowy, imagined guard was nothing more than elements of other people's costumes slung on a pole. Had she been meant to think that?

'Nice dress,' Alex drawled in that smooth Southern accent. She'd begun to wonder if it was put on for the ladies. 'Shows off your assets to their best advantage. Not surprising young Nick hired you.'

Jenna scowled. She hated it when people passed comments like that. Of course, she wouldn't have wished herself plain-faced or flat-chested for the world. But Nick had given her the job because she was good, she was creative, she made things happen. Hadn't he? There was always a niggling doubt. And enough truth in Alex's back-handed compliment to needle her.

He smiled – but the smile didn't reach his eyes – as if he knew he'd hit a raw nerve. God, he was so like Nick! So bloody manipulative. But that tray of food looked good.

Alex sat down on the ground in front of her and laid the tray between them. 'I've already eaten,' he said. 'Enjoy.'

When Jenna hesitated over what to choose first he picked up a small chipolata and offered it to her lips. It was still warm from wherever it had been cooked. Barbecued? It had that smoky flavour. It oozed with juice as she bit into it. There was something so sensual in the way the meaty texture yielded on her tongue. It was spicy, but not too spicy. Middle Eastern style, she guessed. He carried on feeding her.

She wasn't quite sure why. Her hands weren't tied, he could see that. But she didn't protest. There was something a little edgy about being in this position.

Being fed by a man's hands. Feeling his fingers brush her lips as he slipped in piquant Greek sausages, felafel laced with fragrant cumin, mini onion bhajis dipped in tangy mint yoghurt sauce.

Because her hands weren't tied she let them explore. She began tracing the curves of Alex's bare head. Was baldness sexy? She'd never believed that before. But then she'd never tried to touch it. There was something sensual about such naked skin. Something so personal. A new sensation. There seemed so little between her fingerprints and his very thoughts.

The food was finished. It took the edge off her immediate hunger but she wasn't full. She couldn't help feeling a little more would have been nice after the hours of solitude and uncertainty she'd had to endure. The sharp yoghurt sauce wasn't finished, though. Alex dipped his fingers in it and made her lick them clean. He pushed one finger deep into her mouth, probing, exploring. He stroked the insides of her cheeks, the roof of her mouth, the sensitive margins where her teeth met her gums. She'd never appreciated before what a sensuous experience this could be. By the time the sauce pot was empty her whole mouth felt tingling and alive.

'We have unfinished business,' Alex said, and the surrealness of their situation reared up and confronted her. He was an important business contact. A potential investor. She was supposed to impress him but keep him at arm's length. 'Don't cross the line,' as Nick had said to her. And yet the first time they'd found themselves alone she'd let him rub himself off between her breasts. And here he was again staring unashamedly at her exposed twin beauties. How could the three of them work comfortably together after this? Would things at Treganza Leisure International ever be the same after this weekend?

'Got nothing to say for yourself?' Alex challenged. 'Surely you ain't going to claim some sort of loyalty to Nick? He sure don't feel none to you. Face it, honey, you're a married man's bit on the side. You could do better than that jerk.'

'If you think he's such a jerk why did you come here? Why are you considering doing business with him?'

'You don't have to like someone to work with them. You do, after all.'

Jenna bit her lip. She certainly didn't love Nick. No illusions there. Half the time she didn't even like him. He could be pig-headed, a user and compulsively unfaithful. He might be sexy and have a great body but when the mood took him he could be totally selfish in bed. But he could be witty and dynamic, too. He got things done. He was the kid from the wrong side of town who'd made good. Underneath the chutzpah was a vulnerable boy, and Jenna felt a sneaking tenderness for him.

'Don't judge Nick,' she snapped, 'or me. You know nothing about us.'

'I know Nick Treganza's got something I want. Coupla things, actually.' He reached across and touched first one exposed breast then the other. 'How about you come and work for me, Jenna? I'm all set to expand again.' He chuckled. 'The business, I mean. I need someone like you. We could have fun. Don't tell me you ain't tempted.'

She smacked his hand away. 'My services aren't for sale.'

'Sure. You're too busy giving them away.'

That did it. She brought back her hand to slap him round the face.

Alex caught it in mid air. Then the other. 'If you're going to play rough games, little lady, you should have a care who you're playing them with.'

She struggled to free her arms. Too late. His physical strength was the original immovable object. She thought back to the first night here, admiring the muscular tone of his body, assuming that someone who owned a string of health clubs Stateside must work out a lot himself. Now she could feel the results.

In one fluid, seemingly effortless movement Alex pulled her over his lap. She felt gravity do its work and the length of chain around her hips parted, revealing her bare ass. She twisted her hips from side to side but it only made the chains slip apart even more.

'Feel free to struggle,' Alex commented. 'Won't do you a bit of good but I like to see it. Makes the whole thing so much more exciting.'

'You bastard,' she muttered into the unyielding curve of his thigh. He'd engineered this. She was certain. He'd provoked her to attack him first so he could manoeuvre her into this position. And to think just moments ago he'd stimulated the inside of her mouth so unexpectedly, so tenderly, so sensually. Which was the real Alex?

He began to stroke the smooth curve of her buttock. But she knew what was coming next. She braced herself for it.

'Ain't it just the whitest thing?' Alex murmured. 'Never sees the light of day, I'll bet. Not outside, at any rate. You ought to sunbathe in the buff.'

'I like my skin the way it is,' she muttered through gritted teeth. 'Cancer-free.'

'You could be a sensible girl and still have a tush as honey-coloured as the rest of you. Seriously, think about coming over to Texas and soaking up a few of our rays.' He paused. 'Or maybe there's another way to get some colour in those cheeks.'

He spanked her. She'd been expecting it to hurt. It didn't. Jenna gave a little gasp of surprise.

Alex chuckled. 'First time anyone's done that to you? Lady, if your ass wasn't meant to be spanked it wouldn't be so round and fleshy and just made to absorb impact. Relax and learn to be a good girl.'

He spanked her several times more. It was true. It was as if her buttocks were made to absorb the ripples that spread out from the slap of his palm. Alex was clearly an expert at this. He knew just where to spank. Just the right amount of pressure. The perfect tempo. Little waves of sensation flowed from the point of impact and buried themselves deep inside. They shivered up her quim. In its own way, this was heaven. It was more extreme, but just as sensual, as his probing finger in her mouth.

Jenna slumped, passive, on his lap and let the delicious sensations go on. Oh, this was special. This could only be shared by two. She was perfectly capable of pleasuring herself with a finger or vibrator but this – this was a delight she could never recreate alone.

'Had enough yet?' Alex murmured.

'No!' she replied but part of her meant yes. This was almost as good as sex. It was a full-on physical pleasure. She'd like it to go on and on. But it was teasing, too. Although it took her to the edge and held her there she knew she'd never come this way.

Alex paused and slipped a hand between her thighs. She opened them for him.

'Your pussy's juiced up, ma'am,' he said, fingering her. 'May I offer my services?'

Echoes of his previous barb weren't lost on her. She felt a frisson of annoyance shiver through her. He was like Nick – needle, needle, needle. But he was hopefully like him in other ways, too.

'Yes,' she moaned as she raised herself up on to all fours.

Alex wriggled out from underneath her and pulled his shirt off quickly. Then he wrestled his trousers down to his knees. She'd seen his cock before, when it had jousted with her slippery breasts the night before last. Now it stood high and ready again.

He twisted round and, without further preliminaries, entered her from behind. His cock slid in, following and filling the hungry ache his expert spanking had created. Jenna sighed.

'Wish we were doing this in front of a mirror,' Alex grunted. 'The sight of your big firm beauties jumping and jiggling would make me come in no time. What d'you say we make a date for my next trip? I'm going to be visiting England pretty regular from now on.'

Jenna didn't answer. But her head was filled with the possibilities. All these men. All these different chemistries. All these different candidates for sex. Why shouldn't she have it all and not feel guilty?

Alex reached round and grasped her breasts. They were swinging low through the gaping chains and, framed by their cold, silvery links, looked even bigger than ever when she glanced down at them. She was proud of her body. The sight of it turned her on so much. Alex moulded and fondled her breasts, drawing out her nipples and rolling them with the same precision he seemed to apply to everything. She let him do it – simply enjoying his thrusting – for a few moments longer. It was so sweet. But it wasn't quite enough. Her clit was aching. And the swelling of his cock told her he was close to climax himself.

She moaned, unwilling to break the spell by putting her need into words. But Alex understood. He took one hand off her breast and pressed a finger against her hungry clit. Just a little pressure but it was enough to send her over the edge. All the while she cherished his vigorous thrusting as her orgasm bloomed and shivered deep into her.

Alex moved both hands back to her breasts. With this extra tactile excitement he came very soon. She felt his cock rear huge in its climax and burst into her.

Jenna slumped face down on the dry grass floor of the tent. It had been crushed by their bodies and smelled summery and sweet. She heard the sounds of Alex dressing – the rustle of material and the zip of his fly – but she didn't turn and look up at him. She felt suddenly sleepy.

'I meant it about the mirror,' Alex called from the direction of the tent flap. 'Next time I'm in your country, huh?'

Jenna couldn't remember if she answered him.

She must have slept. She had a lot to catch up on and a good, deep orgasm always made her drowsy. Next time Jenna raised her head it seemed to be getting dark.

As she sat up she rubbed her neck muscles. They were stiff from having slept in such an awkward position. And the chain dress was uncomfortable: its links had pressed into her. She took it off.

Yes, it was definitely getting dark. That was August for you. It was the first today, wasn't it? Hottest time of the year but the nights inexorably drawing in. The first of August? Damn – Nick's birthday! She hadn't even been there to say 'Happy Birthday' after all this. Then she noticed something else. It seemed very quiet outside the tent.

She opened the flap. No one around. She lifted a cloak down from the pole – her shadow-guard of the afternoon – and wrapped it round her shoulders. The evening was still sultry but she'd had enough of being on display for the moment. She stepped out into the clearing.

There was a figure crouched at the far end. A male figure. He was arranging sticks for a fire. In the gathering shadows she couldn't be sure but when he looked up she knew she'd been right. Robin.

She came and knelt down opposite him across the unlit fire. He struck a match and they looked at each other through its small yellow flame.

'Where is everyone?' she asked.

'Gone back to the hotel. You can go too if you like. Your choice.'

She reached across and touched his neat, springy beard.

Chapter Eleven

NICK LOOKED OUT of the window. It was getting dark. And . . . he could hardly believe it. A straggling line of people was heading back over the sweeping lawns from the direction of the woods. Most were carrying torches.

His eyes picked out individuals: Eleni, Lisette and was that Jenna? Maybe not. And what the hell had they been doing when this was meant to be his party?

That thought kept coming back to haunt him. His party. His show. But he'd been forgotten. Something else was going on. Someone had left him out of the joke. He bunched his fists at his sides in humiliation. And as he did so he felt the stirring of interest in his crotch. He couldn't be sure if it was his anger or the sense of humiliation that had set it off. It felt good, though.

He was going to find someone. Jenna, preferably. He was going to demand what the hell was going on. She'd give him answers. Especially if he teased her with the Eleni possibility. Then, afterwards, if she was feeling suitably contrite and compliant . . . The warm feeling in his crotch swelled to more than merely interest.

Nick flung open his bedroom door and stamped down the landing towards Jenna's room. He was feeling really upbeat about himself. Really virile.

He hadn't bargained on Lisette intercepting him at the head of the stairs.

'Nick. How convenient. I was just coming to look for you.'

Lisette. She'd do as well as Jenna. Either way. After all, she was his wife.

'Where have you been all this time? What the fuck's happening? This bloody party's been a fiasco. What will people think? That the head of a European leisure chain can't even keep his own birthday bash under control?'

'The only person who is peeved, Nicholas, is you.' At times like this her French accent irritated the hell out of him. It made her sound so superior, so cool. 'Now get back to *our* room.'

She'd stressed the 'our'. And Lisette didn't order him about. Ever. She manipulated. She put on subtle pressure. He was supposed to second guess her half the time. That had been a direct order. Without even a 'please'. Nick was so shocked he complied before he'd realised it. And the whipcrack of authority in her voice had quite excited him.

Lisette closed the door behind them and deliberately locked it.

'You mind telling me what this is all about?' Nick was less sure of himself now. He was concerned to hear it in his own voice. He knew his cock was wilting.

Lisette advanced on him. There was something different about the way she was moving tonight. Powerful. Sure of herself. Sexy. He backed away from her without realising it. He tripped and landed on the bed.

'Husband,' Lisette purred, 'when was the last time we had what you English so quaintly refer to as conjugal rights?'

Nick grinned. He knew he wasn't in a very strong position here – an undignified sprawl on the bed. Lisette wouldn't have been his first choice. But there was something unpredictable about her tonight. He had a feeling he was going to like it.

With one assertive movement she kicked off her high-heeled sandal, rucked her full skirts up above her knee and placed her bare foot down on the duvet beside him.

'You can start by kissing my toes.'

Humour her, Nick thought. Who knows where the game might end? It could be fun.

He rolled on to his side and began kissing where her big toe and second toe met. He'd expected the taste or scent to be acrid. It wasn't. It was . . . mossy, indefinable. Intriguing.

He began kissing round to the side of her foot. He'd never done that before. Now he began to ask himself why. The skin on the vulnerable curve of her high instep was silky, cool. Deliciously kissable. He worked his way over her ankle bone, exploring the contrasts, the mounds, the hollows, the tight Achilles tendon. Lisette's skin was so soft, so cared-for. Hell, this was his wife! He'd never noticed these things about her before. Or about any woman. What else had he been missing?

Nick kissed his way up her inner calf. Lisette moved fully on to the bed and hitched her ruffled skirts up to her hips. She opened her legs for him.

Nick trailed his tongue a little on her warm skin. He nibbled and blew on the tiny whorls his tongue had made. Lisette moaned and lay back. Her expression had lost its habitual studied, slightly bored composure. She was biting her lip and panting. Lisette never responded to him like this!

The thought excited Nick. His excitement went straight to his groin. He was crouched at an awkward angle and his sudden erection felt trapped in his tight trousers. He shifted, reached down and unzipped his own flies giving his penis room to grow. As he lifted his head a little he thought he saw Lisette smile.

He moved on upwards, mouthing his way along her inner thigh. Here Lisette's skin was most velvety of all. Her scent was musky and pinpricked his nostrils. She was wearing tight, dusky pink satin briefs. She opened her legs wider. He pressed his face into that delectable triangle and drank her in.

Nick rarely went down on a lover. If he did it was with a sense of duty. There was no duty about the way he inhaled Lisette's muskiness tonight. No duty at all. He could sense that this was going to be a new beginning.

He didn't remove her briefs at first. He was going to tease her. Though often hell bent on his own sexual pleasure he knew he could be a virtuoso lover when the need called. He ran his tongue up and down the little valley of her labia in the slippery material. Her love juices seeped through the satin. She moaned low again. Sex with Lisette had always seemed functional. A necessary conjugal right – as she'd put it. Nick had always felt she was holding something back. Now she seemed genuinely aroused.

He rubbed his nose into the satiny, slick valley. He

nudged the very tip into her pert clitoris. Lisette groaned louder – something he couldn't quite make out and probably in French. That was always a good sign. She wriggled her thighs, trapping him between them. He was bathed in her utterly female scent.

And he really was trapped. Lisette's thigh muscles were stronger than they looked. She had him pinned by the upper arms. He couldn't reach up and remove her panties. He couldn't put a hand down and comfort his own aching cock which had forced its way out of his boxer shorts and was begging to be rubbed. He could only keep tonguing Lisette through her flimsy but definite barrier.

He worked on her more frantically, lapping at her clitoris through the fabric. She was moaning and pressing her thighs against him even tighter. The pressure was almost pain. He pushed with his tongue, exploring how much the delicate panties would give. More than he had thought at first. He managed to push them into the well between her labia – juiced up and slick with her own arousal. He poked his tongue as far into her as it would go.

Lisette gasped. This was a tease too much for her, evidently. She reached down herself and undid the tie-sides to her briefs, pulling them away and giving him freer access to her springy pubic bush and beyond.

His lips finally made contact with her full, fleshy lips. He kissed them like a mouth. He slipped his tongue deep inside. He rolled and writhed it as if he was French kissing. She was gasping and clasping him even closer with her thighs. Her juice was fresh and sweet and copious on his tongue. Her nether lips were like delicious, tempting morsels for him to taste.

Nick realised he'd never had so much fun performing oral sex. Certainly never on his wife.

But his own need was driving him crazy. The more Lisette wriggled and moaned the more the thought of her arousal pumped up his. The tension in his balls was unbearable. He tilted his hips a little and tried to rub the tip of his cock against the duvet, desperate for release.

Then Lisette began to scream and thrash her legs. He thrust his tongue in deep. He could feel the muscles of her quim pulse sweetly against his pressed mouth as she came.

Nick raised his head. Lisette relaxed her strangling thigh-grip on his body. He raised himself up and gazed at her as her breathing slowed back down to normal. She looked like he'd never seen her look before.

After a long moment she smiled. 'Husband, it's your turn.'

She swung off the bed and began to undo her full, flouncy dress. It fell off her shoulders and towards the floor, sliding slowly and crumpling with the whisper that only quality clothing makes. She was naked beneath.

Nick stared at her breasts. Pendulous – had he ever called them that? They were magnificent. Statuesque. He wondered if she would order him to lie down and dominate him, crowing over him and dangling those heavy breasts in his face. He hoped she would.

Lisette walked slowly towards him. There was power and confidence in every tiny movement of her naked form. She bent over him and began to unbutton his shirt. Her mobile breasts brushed his face. Nick's cock had flagged a little from lack of attention. It sprang up ramrod stiff again.

Having removed his shirt she turned her attention lower down. She slipped off his trousers and then, with difficulty, his boxer shorts. His cock was poking through the slit in the front and, in all its swollen glory, held things up.

What now? Nick wondered. There were two obvious directions this game could take. She might kneel down and suck his cock. Eleni had the better technique, but the novelty of the situation appealed to Nick. Or she could order him flat on his back and go on top. The mood Lisette was in tonight he decided this was the most likely option.

Lisette wasn't playing the same game. 'On all fours,' she ordered and it took Nick a second or two to realise she meant him. Meanwhile she reached for one of her many bags.

Nick did what she told him. Then he looked over his shoulder. Lisette had produced a large, black, double-ended dildo. And she was anointing one end of it with massage lotion.

The shock in his face must have been readable because she laughed.

'As you know, *chèri*, I'm juicy enough already but I thought you'd need a little more help. Especially if this is your first time. It is your first time, isn't it?'

Nick didn't say anything. His insides were churning. She was going to use that thing on him? Where did Lisette get something like that anyway? How long had she been planning this?

He watched her slide one end of the huge dildo into herself. She closed her eyes and sighed. This was deep, slow satisfaction, but Lisette was totally in control. It wasn't the helpless need he'd aroused in her with his tongue. It was something more active. And the size of that thing! Nick felt almost insufficient, though he knew he was more than adequately endowed. His confused cock began to wilt again. Much more of this and he'd be out of action for tonight.

Lisette cradled the dildo inside her as she mounted the bed and knelt behind him. She looked like some freakish hermaphrodite, with her pale skin, her dark African phallus and her enormous breasts. She leant over and whispered in his ear, 'Yes, Nick, I imagine this is your first time. I'm sure you have no idea what it feels like to be fucked.'

With that she penetrated him.

He was too amazed to offer any resistance. Part of him didn't want to. Part of him was curious. And Lisette had been thorough with the lubricating massage lotion. She seemed to know what she was doing. Nick began to suspect he didn't quite know everything about his wife.

She rode him slowly, taking her time. Nick felt like he'd never felt before. There had been the twins and the end of the riding crop, but that was nothing like the stretching sensation he felt now. The penetration filled a profound need he hadn't even known was there. And more than that. On a purely physical level her pliable shaft was touching that deep, hidden, secret spot inside a man – another trigger of joy. A man could come that way. He'd read about it. He'd just never thought it would happen to him. Lisette moved precisely. She stimulated his hidden hot-spot as if she knew exactly what she was doing. Nick's tortured cock began to stiffen again.

It was an amazing sensation. His cock was growing plumper and meatier by the second without being rubbed. He'd never been aroused in quite this manner. From the growing tension in his balls and the tingling that chased up and down the length of his shaft he felt sure he was building up to an ejaculation. But what would this one feel like?

Lisette adjusted her position. She leant further forwards and he could feel her swinging breasts nudge against his back. Then she bent closer, wrapped her arms round him and squeezed his nipples. He'd fucked women in that position, too – done the exact same thing. The thought added an addictive piquancy.

She rolled both his nipples. She caught them between the ends of her long, manicured fingernails. Yes, she knew what that did to him. She knew what turned him on though she'd never taken the initiative before. The pleasure-pain of it added an extra tremor to his straining cock.

He could hear the note of her breathing change. That little grunt as the breath caught in her throat. She did that when she was close to orgasm. Nick began to shake. Was this her plan? To take her satisfaction then leave him helpless with frustration?

Nick did the reverse of everything he'd ever done when he'd tried to spin it out and prove himself a stud. He thought dirty thoughts. He thought of Jenna, of the redheads, of Eleni's huge pillow breasts where he could bury his face and sigh. But something else drove those soft images out. The spice of humiliation.

He thought of everyone he knew watching him now. He imagined they were doing this in the Treganza Leisure boardroom where he'd so enjoyed laying the compliant Jenna. But he was on the bottom now. In his head and in his body Nick was being uncompromisingly shafted.

The spasm welled up in his balls and flooded through his cock. He was coming and coming all over the duvet and it seemed as if he was never going to stop.

Heather had left a note for Nick at the front desk. It seemed a coward's way out, but she couldn't cope with a scene. Worse, she couldn't cope with there not being a scene because Nick was busy with his important party guests and didn't have time for his kid sister's moods. No, on reflection it wasn't cowardly.

Nick,

Sorry to dip out on the party. Thanks for asking me and all that. I've had a great time. But I need to get away for a bit. About ballet school: I don't think I'll be going back. I know it's what you all wanted for me – right back as far as I can remember. So I suppose I never thought I'd be doing anything else. But now I have thought – and it's just not me. Need to get my head sorted. Be in touch soon.

Love, H x

Sisterly duty done, Heather had more pressing matters on her mind. Like standing in a dim-lit storeroom and wearing only wispy black crotchless panties and a bra Liam had produced from somewhere. She'd never worn crotchless panties before. They made her feel wanton. And the bra fitted so well. It pushed her tight young breasts up and together, giving her the sort of cleavage she could easily get used to.

'Where d'you find them?' she'd demanded as Liam helped her step into the naughty panties that felt as if she wasn't wearing anything even when they were on.

'Room 34. The woman in there had pretty hot taste in lingerie. Helping myself to her undies was quite a turn on. You just let me know when you want anything else.'

'Behave!' She slapped his butt. Liam was already dressed in his biking leathers. She let her hand linger on his tight, leather-clad ass. It was a mind-blowing, sexy texture. She hadn't got blasé about it yet. She walked her hand round to the front of his trousers and felt the tense outline of his balls in the black hide. Then further upwards to his swelling cock.

'A spot of kleptomania turning you on?' she teased. 'Or something else?'

The Heather of forty-eight hours ago wouldn't have said that. She loved the sounds of the words as they tumbled out of her mouth.

'Search me,' he said as he began to kiss the side of her neck. 'Could be that a pint-sized nympho is standing there wearing nothing but two or three ounces of lace when she should be getting dressed in her leathers or it could be that for some reason said nympho can't seem to keep her hands off my cock. C'mon. Let's get moving.'

Reluctantly she stopped feeling up his leather-clad groin and picked up the biking gear Liam had managed to borrow for her. She slipped it straight on over her underwear. She wanted to feel the animal hide with its distinctive fragrance against her own skin. The trousers, when she stepped into them and eased them over her thighs, were tight even on her slim body. Heather felt well and truly bound.

The four seams that met at the crotch nudged her labia through the gap in the lace. She knew her own musky juices must be mingling with the leather scent. How would Liam react if she held that leather and its sexy cocktail against his face? That could be a game for later . . .

She loved the jacket with its buckles and chunky steel zip. The straps reminded her of being tied up.

'When we get where we're going . . . Where *are* we going, by the way?'

'Cornwall. Just outside Bodmin. We're doing this medieval fayre in some castle. The boss's uncle's setting it up. I told you he'd stretched himself thin to take this job. What were you going to say?'

'When we get where we're going I want you to tie me up again. But I'm going to struggle. You might need some help to do it.'

He kissed her, his tongue snaking deep into her mouth as if to print his dominance upon her.

'Jeez, I've created a monster. C'mon now. Quicker we get there, quicker I'll be able to satisfy your deeply depraved fantasies. Don't worry - Cornwall's not far. Not when I ride that thing like a maniac.'

He handed her a spare helmet and they went out into the night.

The motorbike was standing under a high-powered security light. When Liam sat astride and gunned it into life it had a low, throaty rumble. Even the sound was sexy. It seemed to vibrate right through Heather where she stood and made her feel hot again. Liam walked the bike around. She threw her leg over the back and snuggled close behind him.

She remembered being behind Alex on the horse just the day before. But that had been a slow, sensual rhythm. This was going to be the ride of her life.

Liam revved the engine once more. The bike rumbled out of the yard, round the side of the dark, oppressive Hall and crunched along the sweeping gravel drive towards the road. When they hit the dark, smooth tarmac Liam let the powerful engine go. Heather gasped. It was like the G-force pull of an airplane take-off. More – every second was taking her further and further away from brooding Netherdean Hall. She had experienced a beginning there. But now she was speeding towards the future.

Their full-beam headlamp was the only light on the twisting country lane. But she could barely see it – her visor had a smoky tint and Liam's shoulders blocked her view. With the unfamiliar, bulky helmet muffling her from the world outside all she could hear was the roar of the engine. And that was more a vibration, coming straight into her body, by-passing her ears.

Sensory deprivation was unfamiliar. She couldn't even talk to him – though they were so close her breasts pressed firmly into his back. Movement was the only sensation that seemed to mean anything. 'Let yourself go,' Liam had told her when first explaining about riding pillion. 'Don't try to balance independently. You'll only end up fighting me. Just sit loose. Go with the flow.'

It was like surrendering to him utterly. Liam barely slowed for the frequent twists and switchbacks on the unlit road. They took corners with the bike leaning at crazy angles. She had to fight her own instincts to do as Liam had told her and not resist. But she did it. She went with the flow although her heart was racing with fear. And something else apart from fear. It was exciting. She was trusting this black leather speed demon she barely knew with her life. It was the ultimate physical submission.

And Heather was feeling so utterly physical tonight. So completely in her body. The body she'd berated for so long for being itself, for craving sweet things, for gaining the tiniest roll of flesh, for failing to make the perfect leap every time. She was learning to love it now.

The evening was still hot, and she'd declined black leather gauntlets like Liam's. Now she slipped one hand from Liam's waist for a moment and unzipped her jacket halfway down. An unexpectedly cold draft whipped in, funnelling down her cleavage and making her flesh tingle. But she felt so alive. She wanted more. The wispy black bra cups were scantier than she was used to. They barely covered her nipples as it was. She worked them free. Her nipples tensed in the whistling night air.

Liam's leather jacket had his name spelt out in nub-like metal studs across the back. If Heather shifted just a little she could grind her breasts against them. The coldness of the metal. The raw texture of the leather, scuffed and rougher here and there where Liam had evidently gambled a bend and lost. That, too, gave a hint of danger. She could be on the edge of life. It gave everything she felt an added spice.

Heather carried on rubbing her half-bare breasts against Liam's studded back. She was seriously horny now. But what effect was it having on him?

Her right hand round his waist slipped lower. She stroked his taut thigh. She found the inner seam of his trousers and traced it up to his groin.

She loved the feel of his balls and cock encased in leather. She was sure she'd read somewhere that you could get special condoms made from calf skin. Liam would know. She'd love to feel him wearing one.

For a moment she just ran her middle finger tip up and down the outline of his cock. He was hardening. She was sure. She wanted to feel him in her hand – bare skin against moistening bare skin. She undid the chunky press stud at his waist and tried to ease down the heavy brass zip of his flies. But it wasn't just his prick that was stiff tonight.

It was impossible in that position to unzip them. The angle was wrong. The zip wouldn't budge. Liam didn't slow the bike or make the slightest move to help her.

She knew he was hot. She knew he was hard for her. She so wanted to set his erection free in the night air. The ultimate high: sex and speed. She would have rubbed him lovingly as he snaked and leaned into the bends at over a hundred miles per hour. He could have come all over the powerful engine and her hands.

As it was she could barely slip one finger in and touch the cramped tip of his cock. His foreskin was warm and mobile and moist for her. For a moment she couldn't help thinking of Robin and his pierced cock. What that would have felt like in her hands. If he joined them in Bodmin as he'd promised to do . . . well, she'd told Liam he might need some help tying her up.

The bike roared on. They joined a wider road, flashed through a midnight town, climbed a hill the other side. Finally, on the brow of the hill and with the amber glow of the town still bathing them he brought the bike to an abrupt halt, tyres screaming on the dusty tarmac. He walked the bike a little off the road. Then he took off his helmet and shook out his hair.

'You win,' he said in the soft Irish lilt Heather couldn't help but find seductive. 'I can't concentrate on two things at once.'

Heather took off her own helmet. She was very aware that sweat had plastered her fair hair to her neck. Now she had her helmet out of the way she realised there was a half moon risen above them. It gave more light than she would have thought. The air was still now. It was all such a contrast to the rush and roar of the bike. Another pace, another reality.

Liam turned to her. She brushed his darker, damp hair back from his forehead and his neck. She drew his sharp-featured, good-looking face down to hers and kissed him. He shot his tongue deeply into her mouth. She loved the roughness of it snaking into her. But she needed more. His dominant kiss made her sex pulse in response.

'Take me over the bike,' she whispered. 'Take me over the hot engine.'

Liam grinned. 'Hot yourself. I've got a better idea. Sit astride me.'

Reluctantly – she'd come to love the powerful beast between her legs – Heather dismounted. Liam stripped off his leather trousers and wriggled backwards on the bike. His erection was standing up high against the little curls of dark pubic hair that trailed up towards his navel. She could see the cool moonlight gleaming on the moist, eager tip of his cock.

'I see you've made a start,' he said, eyeing her gaping, unzipped jacket and the disarrayed bra with her nipples peeping over the top. 'Get your trousers off, then. Come and ride me.'

The tight leather jeans had become like a second skin moulded to her body's warmth. She peeled them down with difficulty. She left the black crotchless panties on, though. Then she advanced on him.

'No,' she insisted as Liam took one hand in the fingers of the other to pull his gauntlets off. 'Leave them. I want you to touch me up with them on.'

Facing him, she mounted the bike. She unclipped the front of her bra, and Liam closed his gauntleted hands on her breasts. In the heavy gloves his fingers were thick. They looked huge, like a giant's paws. As he squeezed her breasts the thought kept looping through her head, 'A giant is going to be fucking me.' The image stirred her. There was no more need for foreplay. Heather knew she was damp. The scent of her own readiness, now laced with the tang of leather, wafted up through the sultry night. She knew she was wet. She glanced down at Liam's cock. His ramrod erection was just about visible in the moonlight but she could feel its hardness against her mons. She could feel its heat. He was ready, too. Why wait?

Heather shifted her position, raised her hips and brought them down again, welcoming Liam's stiff organ deep into her willing sex. In this position – with her on top, her in control – he slid in deep. He was so thick, so sure. Taking up just the space she wanted him to take, reaching in, feeding her crying need. She loved the feel of his cock. At that moment she never wanted to be without it.

'Ride me,' Liam moaned. 'Start riding me or I'll go crazy.'

Smiling at the pleading note in his voice, Heather began to move. This was even better than the sensation of being filled. In this position her clitoris ground against the angle where the root of his cock met his springy pubic thatch. Every tiny movement was a pleasure. Every tiny movement kept up the delicious pressure on her clitoris – the hungry, demanding seat of her joy. This was divine sex. This was powerful. And there was almost nothing to it! She just had to keep rocking and grinding like this.

She was driving Liam out of his head. She knew it. Her subtle little dance wasn't the all-out, animal thrusting that came instinctively to a young, horny male. But at the same time he must be loving her slow torture. His cock up inside her was so hard, so snug. She could feel every inch of its length.

Heather carried on selfishly taking her own pleasure from his erection. He felt like her prisoner. His oversized paws were still busy on her breasts, nipping her peaked nipples between his fore and middle fingers. The touch of leather again. It fired up her excitement.

She began to move a little faster. Instinct drove her movements as the buzz in her fleshy mons told her that her orgasm was building. She felt a revving in her body – a change of gear as if she were the powerful motorbike he was handling. Only she was in control. She called the shots, the pace at which this pleasure mounted. The slow, sweet build up. And then she felt the now familiar tingle rising, becoming stronger, maturing into a clasping orgasm.

In its wake her quim was still delectably sensitive. She revelled in the sensations as she slammed her body up and down on Liam's, giving him the fast and furious stimulation she knew he needed to come. He wasn't long. He cried and leather-gripped her breasts as she felt his warm explosion in her sex.

Afterwards, panting, he whispered into her neck, 'Now can we get to Cornwall? While I still have a job?'

The moon had dipped below the highest branches of the trees and now there was less light. Heather groped on the ground for her helmet and leather trousers. Liam nodded to her bra and jacket which were still undone. 'Zip up,' he said. 'It gets pretty draughty in front.'

'What?'

'You heard. While we're still on the quiet roads you can have a go in the driver's seat.'

She gunned the bike into life again as Liam showed her. With her lover nestled in close behind her Heather gave a whoop as she headed into the dark, to Cornwall and the future.

Chapter Twelve

THE CRACKLING LIGHT from the fire he'd just lit was playing eerie tricks with Robin's good looks. But then firelight always did that, Jenna thought. With his dark hair, clipped beard and almost-naked torso the flames should have made him look devilish. But it was a sad, reflective sort of devil who cupped her hand and pressed the palm against his lips.

After a long time he murmured, 'This has all got out of control.'

Out of control. That's what Nick had said to her on the first night. Forty-eight hours and a whole world away.

'What do you mean?'

'I was naïve. I thought I could hide behind my role and pull the strings. Be the mischief maker. Mischief was all it was ever meant to be. But the whole thing's got its own dynamic. I hadn't figured there would be others out to get Nick. I should have known, shouldn't I? He was always the type to piss people off.'

A coldness tightened just under Jenna's solar plexus. Out to get Nick? She'd been a play-prisoner here since the previous evening. What had happened in that time? If Treganza Leisure International was in trouble . . . She shook her head. It wasn't just her job. The last two years' experience meant she could walk into another any time she liked. There had been regular offers. Most of them more subtle than Alex Dumont's. No, it was Nick. She felt absurdly protective and it took her by surprise.

'Nick's going to be okay? Robin . . . ?'

'Nick's going to learn a lesson. One he's had coming for a long time. He can take care of himself.' Robin sighed and looked round at the medieval tents and paraphernalia. Some of the tents were beginning to lean and slump towards the earth. 'I'd better start getting cleared up. This is the downside. The unglamorous bit. We need to shift all this stuff to Bodmin first thing tomorrow or I'll be leaving one uncle in the lurch.'

He let go of her hand. He'd been holding it a long time, Jenna realised. There was something touchingly innocent about it.

Just as he was about to straighten up there was a rustle in the leaf litter by their feet. His snake. Robin reached his hand down and the creature curled sinuously up his arm. Jenna touched its muscular coils. It was fascinating – the way it moved, moulded itself to the warmth of his body. She could almost be converted.

'Lilith,' she said, stroking the patterned scales on the back of the creature's neck.

'You remembered.'

'The second. That implies there was a Lilith the First.'

'There was.'

'If you'd rather not tell me . . .'

'No. I will. I should. We were camping – all of us. That last summer before it all went wrong. I was eight – nearly nine. About five o'clock in the morning Lilith crept into the wrong sleeping bag. Hell, she was just a snake. She didn't realise she was doing anything wrong. Just wanted the warmth. But he freaked. Leapt up like she was poisonous. Dragged her outside and smashed her skull on a rock. A snake's nervous system is different to ours. It took her ages to die.' He stroked his living snake tenderly. It began winding itself round Jenna's arm as well, joining them in a smooth, sliding figure of eight. 'I cried. And he made me feel so small and weak and stupid for it. Like always. So it's probably the last time I ever did.'

Jenna reached to touch his face again. To say . . . she didn't know what. Or rather she did. There was something she wanted to ask. But at that moment Robin looked up and said, 'Look, the troops have started arriving. It really is time we got things packed up.'

She turned to follow his gaze. The redheaded twins had arrived silently and were standing just where the shifting firelight met the shadows of the wood. They were dressed more practically now: robust jeans and vest-style T-shirts. But it didn't detract from their voluptuous figures one bit. They both had their arms folded as they waited. It lifted and emphasised their welcoming breasts.

Jenna felt a frisson of rising desire as she looked at them. Before this weekend she'd felt guilty for looking at another woman's body like that. Since her adventures with Lisette she wasn't stamping on those feelings so hard. Quite simply, the redheads turned her on. Their curves, their softness, the curiosity they aroused. What would it be like to cup another woman's breasts, rub her own against them, slip them up and down and between?

As if they'd read her thoughts the twins smiled mischievously, in tandem, then turned to look at each other for a moment. Then the nearest said to Robin, 'Boss, it's no big deal. The tents and stuff, I mean. And the rest of the crew'll be here in a minute. We've done this before. We're big strong girls. You get off. You know you want to.'

Robin gathered up Lilith and handed the snake to the girls. 'Keep her safe.' Then he took Jenna's hand and drew her out of the circle of firelight.

'Where to?' she asked.

'Wherever. I've got no agenda. No plan.'

She hadn't expected to see him like this. He seemed vulnerable without a grand plan. She was afraid of his vulnerability. It appealed to her feminine instincts: opened a crack in her own defences. Nick had taught her to keep up her guard. But where was Nick?

Suddenly an idea came to Jenna and she wasn't sure why, except it seemed right for things to come full circle.

'Let's swim. Let's go to the lake.'

Maybe they took a shortcut. Maybe Robin could still surprise her with the way he knew these woods. Or maybe, with familiarity, the landscape had contracted the way landscapes do. Whatever the reason, it seemed only minutes before they were skirting the edge of the old Hall and making their way down to the lake.

They stopped just past the water's edge with the coolness lapping their ankles. Robin undid the borrowed cloak, slipped it from her shoulders then tossed it far on to the bank. Jenna was completely naked underneath. But the night was humid and it felt good. He clasped her shoulders, pulled her against him and kissed her probingly for a long, long time. Then he ran his sensitive fingers down her breasts, her belly, her flaring hips with such attentiveness it was as if he'd never seen them before.

Jenna began to moan and wriggle with impatience. Especially when his deft fingers cupped her breasts and caught her nipples and wouldn't let go. She couldn't wait any longer. It was high time she saw Robin naked.

She eased his leather waistcoat down over his firm, trim deltoids and threw it aside. Here, far from the Hall and its subdued lights, she relied on her sense of touch. She ran her fingertips over his shoulders and warm, sinuous arms. Then round to the front and his chest with its scattering of dark hair and silver nipple ring that gleamed in what little light there was.

Jenna hooked two fingers into his leather waistband. Robin kicked off his sandals – his bare feet were touching hers now. His long toes were roving, exploring as his fingers had done. She'd never thought this could be a sensuous experience. But it was.

She won her brief struggle with his fly-clasp and began to slide the chunky brass zip down. She didn't feel any underwear as she slipped her hands in and around. This didn't surprise her. Robin seemed the type to do without. As she eased his leather trousers further down his hips his cock spilled out. Its pierced tip rested for a moment on the sensitive skin of her forearm. He wasn't fully hard. Not yet. But there was a definite stirring and the silver ring against her smooth wrist began to move.

He grinned. The low light caught against his very white and slightly unmatched teeth flashing through his dark beard. 'You wanted to swim,' he said. 'Let's do it!'

Robin kicked off his trousers and splashed away from her through the lake. He took a long dive, his slender body arching in the air. He came up like a seal and rolled over in the water. It gleamed as it streamed off him. The moon had just cleared the gothic roof of the Hall and its light made his whole damp body look silver.

'Come on,' he called. 'What are you waiting for?'

Jenna didn't know why she'd hung back. Perhaps she was just savouring the moment. Robin and her alone, relaxed and 'no agenda'. She waded towards him. The water held her thighs back. Pond weed tickled her knees. Something brushed against her calf. Tiny fishes? Jenna shuddered. Then she felt an idiot. Lakes and fishes – what was wrong with that? She'd led an indoor life for far too long.

From the deepest part of the lake Robin laughed and splashed her. There was something innocent about his laughter. They were two teenagers larking about. He was no longer the puppet master. Looking at him simply spinning in the water and sending up glittering droplets from his fingertips she wondered if he ever had been.

She went to him. He stopped his wild dancing in the water and pressed his long body against hers. They kissed, searchingly. The contrast of textures confused her senses: the warmth of skin on skin, the coolness of the water, the hardness of his silver body jewellery against her soft chest.

They stood there pressed to one another for a long time. Their bodies seemed to flow together like the water. She wondered if they were becoming indistinguishable. She could feel his cock against her inner thigh – only semi-erect in the cold water, but still a presence.

Robin broke off and she saw him glance up the hill to Netherdean Hall. There were few lights showing.

'Not much of a party happening,' she commented.

'Everyone's exhausted.'

'What's happened, Robin?'

'Even I don't know that.' He grinned teasingly. 'You can go and find out if you're that impatient.'

She punched him in the ribs. 'I'm going nowhere! You know that. Which reminds me, I never made it to the boathouse last night. Someone interrupted me. Let's go and see what plans Nick had.'

The boathouse floor was covered with soft rugs and cushions. There were candles round the edges. Robin found matches and lit them one by one. They dried their damp bodies on some of the velvety throws.

'You're different,' Jenna murmured as they knelt facing each other in a halo of candles.

'From?'

'Different from how you were before. When you kidnapped me. When you kept me in the tent. God, you were an infuriating bastard!'

'That's because this wasn't in the plan. You weren't in the plan – not specifically. Not as you, Jenna. The aim was to make Nick look a fool. Throw a spanner in the works. Make him look like he wasn't in control.

Because that's what matters to him – more than anything.'

'Don't I know it. Let's not talk about him. Robin...' She leant forward and ran a hand up his iron-hard thigh. She took his cock in her hand and it rose willingly under her caress.

It was high and swollen when he laid his hand over hers and said, 'Wait. No hurry, is there. Lie down against those cushions, Jenna.'

She obeyed. Whatever this Machiavellian planner had in mind, she was willing.

'That candlelight's fantastic.' He grinned. 'Accentuates your every curve. Spread your legs for me, Jenna.'

She obeyed him.

'Now play with yourself. Imagine you're horny as hell and haven't had an orgasm for days. Pretend I'm not here. What would you do?'

She hesitated. She'd never masturbated in front of a lover. It seemed too intimate. The last taboo and Robin knew it.

'I'm going to break down your barriers, Jenna. All of them. Go on. Show me how you'd pleasure yourself.'

Break down her barriers. It had a seductive, dangerous sound to it. And the silken way he'd said it with a hint of threat in his voice. The threat that if she didn't do this for him now he'd get up and walk away.

Two days ago she hadn't known Robin. After tonight she might never see him again. There was a safety in strangers. An intimacy that carried no baggage. If she could do it with anyone, she could do it with him.

Jenna began stroking her breasts. She ran her fingers over the upper curves and then down into her cleavage where they fanned out over her breasts. She lingered over this for several minutes, enjoying her bosoms' weight, their suppleness, their proud, thrusting curves. But the sensual tide was rising in her. She was hungry for more. She cupped a breast in each hand, took her nipples between thumb and forefinger and rolled and squeezed them hard.

Robin was sitting back on his heels in front of her. He'd spread his thighs wide. His erection was high and quivering. Obviously he was enjoying this too.

Jenna pinched both nipples as hard as she could without it turning to pain. This was divine. This was what she loved. To have both nipples pleasured at once. This was why it had been so sinfully sweet when Robin had tied her up on the floor and let two men tongue her breasts. This was why almost every woman's fantasy is to have two lovers in her bed.

And then the moment of sweet torture. The dilemma Jenna faced every time she masturbated. Her clitoris was aching with the need to be rubbed. But her nipples demanded stimulation too. She carried on past the moment of sweetness, to the point where her frustrated arousal was practically pain. Her breasts were so responsive, her nipples so sensitive, she'd always wondered if she could achieve orgasm just by fondling them. But she'd never had the patience. She didn't have it now. She abandoned one pouting nipple, reached down with her right hand and toyed with her aching clitoris.

She was close. She knew she was close. Her fingertip was covered with her own slippery juice as she massaged her clitoris. Robin came closer as she rubbed.

He put his palms on her flexed knees and pushed them further apart. She felt her juiced-up labia slip open. He was looking into her intimate self. No barriers.

Jenna struggled against him. Her urge was to press her thighs tighter together at this point. That's what she instinctively did when she pleasured herself. Did Robin know this? Was he teasing her – spinning out the process.

She switched her left hand to her other nipple. It was never enough. She had to weave back and forth between them. She longed to ask Robin to suck one of them. But she knew he wouldn't. That wasn't in the rules.

His arms were forcing her knees apart like a kind of delicious body-bondage. She strained against it but even the straining was erotic. She wanted it, too. She had never come with her muscles working in quite this kind of constriction. And when she finally did she found the way the sensations played tag around the tops of her thighs and over her mons before and afterwards was well, well worth it.

Robin sighed and released her knees. Then he lay down on the blankets and turned over on to his side. 'Lie in front of me,' he said, 'with your back towards me.'

Again she complied. He was the child in the playground who knew all the best games. Had all the best ideas. Robin reached round from behind her and cupped both her breasts. Her nipples were still peaked and raw from the way she'd been rubbing them. Then he eased his cock forward between her thighs as far as it would go.

Robin had a long cock. The end of it protruded stubbily beneath her bush, as if it belonged to her.

'Rub it,' he whispered in her ear. 'Pretend whatever you like.'

Jenna had never had much truck with Freud's 'penis envy'. She'd always been far happier having breasts. And an orgasm that happened deep inside her body. Just this once, though. Just this once she let herself imagine.

She touched the tip – the strange, pierced tip of his cock – as if it was her own. The silver ring was warm. She'd thought the metal might be cold, but no, of course, it was warm from his body heat. As warm as the mobile, tender foreskin that yielded under her curious fingertips. But the ring didn't yield. It seemed the only difference. Otherwise it was like part of him. Or her. Could it move? She slipped it a millimetre or so, tentatively at first.

Robin moaned in her ear, 'Oh Jenna. Yes. It's so sexy when you do that. So sensitive. I can't describe it. It's the sort of sensation you never know until you've had your body pierced.'

She rolled the ring backwards and forwards a little more, testing how much play there was in it. Robin's cock kicked in her hand. His breathing against her neck became ragged. He clenched his fingers fiercely on her soft, heavy breasts. Feeling them was clearly turning him on, too.

Jenna took a firmer grip on the end of his cock. With her thumb on the top of his glans she stroked her fingers along the sensitive underside of his shaft. She could just about reach. A shudder went through Robin's whole body pressed behind her.

His shaft was pressing up firmly between her legs. It nudged against her clitoris. As she stroked its velvety underside and it responded eagerly to her stroking, his flesh pressed harder into her flesh. As she stimulated his cock so her own sexual hot spot was being triggered. It made the link so close. She could fool herself the responsive male organ rearing up between her legs was her own.

Jenna let these wild imaginings off the leash in her head. She was a man. She was a man as sensual and mischievous as Robin with his ever-ready cock. It was magnificent. It was virile. It stood to attention whenever she wanted it to. Women worshipped it. Were falling over each other to welcome it between their legs.

She felt intoxicated by this. The power. No wonder it went to men's heads.

His cock and her clit seemed welded by their own heat. When she caressed one she caressed both. Both responded. His cock was straining higher than ever now – straining towards orgasm. It pressed into her. There was a sudden pulsing and she couldn't tell whether it came from his rod or her sex.

Robin came. His cock jerked and thumped her clitoris as he climaxed in a wide, creamy arc across the boathouse floor. Jenna felt breathless herself. Blood was pounding in her clit, her mons, her labia. She wasn't sure if it was the super-sensitivity still lingering after her first orgasm or whether she'd just come again with him.

They disentangled their bodies. He propped himself up on one elbow and she rolled down and back to look at him.

'It needn't be over,' he murmured. 'I still want to make love to you properly.'

Make love. It wasn't a phrase she'd ever expected to hear him use. Now, suddenly, after their weird almost-melting-into-one it sounded right.

She reached for him – her hands roving over his chest, slipping over his shoulders, his smooth, taut back – to bring him close to her.

'Not here, though,' Robin continued, pulling away from her a little. 'There really is only one place that would make sense.'

By the time they arrived back at the clearing in the woods all evidence of the tents had been packed away. They listened. No one else was around. A few fires were still burning, casting jumbled lights on the undersides of leafy branches overhead. Robin tossed more fallen branches on the hot embers and then the clearing was ablaze again.

As she moved out of the shadows and into the shifting amber bubbles of light Jenna felt they could have been people from almost any point in time. Naked, they'd wrapped blankets from the boathouse round themselves as makeshift cloaks. Just a man and a woman approaching the primitive fire. And the chalky outline of the lion-headed giant in the centre, glowing a little.

'He was never meant to last,' Robin said, clasping both her hands and leading her to stand on the image. 'Let's send him off the way he'd want to go.'

He shrugged the blanket cloak from his own shoulders then unwrapped hers and tossed it aside. They were naked together again.

She caught hold of his neck and pulled him down till they were both kneeling on the crumbly leaf litter. His hands roved over her shoulders, her bare breasts, as sinuously, as gracefully as his snake might have wound itself around her curves. He was in no hurry. He knew her body. He'd been here before. He knew where this was going. There was every reason to linger.

There was a narrow leather thong holding his hair at the nape of his neck. She pulled it free. His long tresses fell into her upturned face, brushing her cheeks like a caress.

His narrow fingers began playing on her naked skin – a rapid, drumming rhythm like a concert pianist with a challenging toccata. It sent little vibrations through her breasts. He spent a long time there – clearly enjoying the sight of the ripples he'd set in motion. Jenna glanced down for a moment. Yes, no question he was enjoying it. Robin's cock was stiffening again.

He moved lower. His fingertips danced over her soft belly. The muscles round her navel tightened in reflex. He probed a middle finger into that whorl of nerve endings. Another passage into the body, sealed off and necessarily virginal, but with an untapped potential for sensuality – as Jenna began to discover.

Robin pressed her body down on to the earth. He continued to cover her stomach with kisses. He paused again and wriggled his tongue into her navel. It fluttered there like a captive bird. Jenna laughed out loud at the feeling. But it was tingling down her nerves, too. Setting up more interesting stirrings lower in her body.

He followed these stirrings, kissing his way over her lower belly, playing with the little snaking trail of her pubic hair until it joined the main luxuriant bush. He combed through it with his nose, drinking in her scent. Then he dipped his tongue between her slick lips.

She was high on anticipation. Shivers ran through

her body, and it vibrated like a railway track when a train approaches. It was finally going to happen. Robin was going to penetrate her with his almost-sacred cock. That thought was all she needed. She was aroused enough; she barely needed his skilful tongue probing her labia, teasing her clitoris. She still revelled in it though, it was an extra treat. Until the peak of her arousal was too achingly close and she wound her fingers into his long dark hair and raised him up.

'Robin. Now.'

'Ride me then, Jenna. Ride me.'

They twisted over, his body surrendering to hers on the soft, sweet-smelling earth. She raised her hips and brought them down slowly, slowly, savouring every second as his cock parted her labia and glided in – stretching her, filling her. He'd entered her. At last. And she was controlling the pace now, controlling the exact angle his long shaft stroked her clitoris.

Jenna swung her breasts into his face. He grasped them, squeezed her nipples tight between his fingers. The circle of pleasure was complete. She knew. She was in for a simple but absolutely perfect fuck.

She closed her eyes, losing herself in the tactile sensations, and time was put on hold. The scent of the dark, damp forest, the woodsmoke and Robin – his exotic, musky oil – filled her. She rolled her hips. Her body rejoiced in their simple contact, his flesh deep inside her flesh. She was so conscious of his erection rearing up inside her that she felt whole.

Instinct took over. She lost herself in an unchoreographed dance – her body knew its own moves. Pure lust. Pure celebration. When she ground her hips in a slow figure of eight roll she wasn't deliberately teasing Robin, though some small, amused, detached part of her knew that was the effect. She was pleasing herself. And she knew this sort of roll would keep a lusty man hard for ages, but not make him come.

But suddenly Robin seized control. His hands released her breasts, grasped the small of her back and – with his cock still rooted in her – flipped her over till she was on her back on the body-warmed earth. Having got her where he wanted he thrust fiercely. She could feel the whole length of his cock burning her sex. He was closer to coming than she was now. She could hear it in his jagged breathing, feel it in the final swell of his cock. She couldn't let that happen.

Jenna gripped his shoulders. She knew Robin had the genuine strength of slender, wiry men. She was only going to get one shot at this. She had to time it right. With every ounce of strength she had, and some she hadn't expected, she pushed and twisted.

They rolled and carried on rolling. Their bodies tumbled and thrashed on the fine leaf litter. Their long, loose hair mingled. If the occasional twig dug into Jenna's soft back she was too high on the struggle to notice the momentary pain. They were joined fast at the groin as if the heat of lust had melted and reformed their bodies.

When the tumble finished Jenna was back on top again. Robin's erection was still firm within her. More breathless than ever from their struggle, he seemed turned on rather than distracted by it. And he was grinning.

'Teach you to change your mind,' she whispered down at him.

He slapped her buttock; Jenna wriggled with the

delicious little ripples of stimulation. 'Teach you to tease my cock,' he whispered back.

She began to ride him again. She was close now and she knew it. Robin's long fingers closed on her nipples again. He caught them in a scissor action – squeezed till he had her on the cusp of pain then squeezed some more. But it wasn't pain by then. It was . . . extreme. She loved it. She needed it.

As he rolled and pinched her nipples she could feel her orgasm priming itself to rise. It began as a series of tingles chasing each other across her labia. Then it plunged deep into her – sharp as a knife but warm, sheer pleasure. It filled her whole lower body. Her muscles pulsed round Robin's cock.

While she was still in the grip of pleasure he seized her and tumbled her over again. This time she yielded unconditionally. He thrust his cock into her at his own ardent pace. In the afterglow of her climax Jenna lay passive and just enjoyed the virile feel of his thrusts. Lying like that she was very aware when his cock gave its final, full to bursting swell, kicked inside her and came.

Robin stayed in her for a long time afterwards. He propped himself up on both elbows. She tucked some of his loose hair back behind his ear. And they looked into each other's eyes, saying nothing. There was a strange intimacy about it. She felt more open, more vulnerable, even, than when they'd been making love.

Finally she looked beyond him to the sky. With a shock she realised it was getting lighter. Not dawn. Dawn was still a fair way off. But the night was almost over.

They rolled away from each other. Jenna felt a

sadness as his cock slid out of her. She wondered if it would ever happen again. Surely, the chances were against it?

And then, by the fading glow of the fires and the growing light above, she noticed the woodland floor beneath their bodies. Their tussles had almost obliterated the priapic giant's proud lines. Another sense of loss, too close on the heels of the first, made Jenna gasp.

'I told you he wasn't meant to last,' Robin said. 'Just think of him as going back underground.'

Jenna felt cold. She reached for her cloak. What on earth would she look like sneaking back to the Hall wrapped only in that? Who would be around to notice?

'I'd better go,' she said. 'I can hear real life calling.'

She'd meant it to sound flippant. Instead it came out sad.

Then, 'Your snake,' she said quickly, because this might well be the last time she'd have the chance. 'The first one. It was Nick who killed her, wasn't it? That's why you hate him.'

Robin nodded. 'Not only that, but it was the most brutal thing. I don't suppose he's changed.'

What was left of the firelight caught a single tear in the corner of his eye. It was probably nothing. Just his eyes watering naturally from a long night without sleep. But on impulse Jenna kissed it away. Its biting saltiness stayed on her lips all the way back to the old Hall.

Chapter Thirteen

NICK WOKE WITH an erection. He reached under the sheet to cradle it lovingly. The day after his thirtieth birthday and the old boy was as virile as ever! He grinned and toyed with the idea of masturbating. His penis seemed so insistent. But then he remembered beginning to masturbate alone in this room before – the two redheads and their snake coming in . . . He'd rather not revisit that.

He'd save himself. It was a long way back to London. Plenty of opportunities for losing some time. He assumed Lisette had already left. Her bags had gone. But he might arrange to meet Jenna somewhere discreet. Or Eleni. He was sure he'd written down her new mobile number.

Nick cupped his balls. Then his fingers wandered further back. He felt a little raw. But in an agreeable way. There was the thrill of newness about it. Perhaps this was how girls felt the morning after they'd lost their virginity?

He and Lisette had phoned room service for champagne the previous night. They'd toasted 'new beginnings' in their relationship. He'd begun to wonder what games they might explore. After all, he'd married an older woman. She'd taken her time getting round to corrupting him but once she'd started, who was he to argue? Nick had begun to get horny again but Lisette had plied him with more champagne and he'd fallen asleep. His head felt a little muzzy now.

He ordered room service to bring him breakfast while he packed. It arrived with a note Heather had asked reception to pass on. What was that girl up to? When he read it he almost choked on his black coffee. Of all the ungrateful . . . He tried her mobile. Several times. On the third attempt a laid-back, male, Irish voice told him Heather was a bit tied up at the moment – before dissolving into giggles.

Whatever performance his little half-sister was putting on Nick refused to let it spoil his mood. He zipped up his bag and left it outside his door ready for a porter. Soon he'd be on his way back to London. He was fired up to do what he was good at: run his company and make money. And as for other things he was good at . . . the shock and surprise of Lisette's behaviour still hadn't worn off. He'd underestimated her. He'd married a fine woman with depths he hadn't begun to explore. It set his pulse racing. As Nick walked out into the car park he felt a lucky man.

The two redheads, dressed in jeans and cut-away T-shirts, were loading the nearest of a trio of large white vans. From time to time they shouted to someone inside. They were strong girls – they hefted boxes and bales of cloth and swung them around like men. Nick nodded in approval. All that physical work must be how they kept their breasts so firm. A warm stirring of appreciation began in his groin.

One of the redheads moved aside and slammed one half of the van's double back door. Nick read:

> Treganza
> Re-enactments
> Entertainments
> limited

Hell, he thought, I own more than I realised. But that lettering isn't company standard. Have to give Jenna a hard time about that. It's her job. She knows how important it is to have an instantly recognisable logo.

He was still grinning over the idea of 'giving Jenna a hard time' when he heard the crunch of footsteps on gravel. He turned. Lisette was coming towards him. So she hadn't already left. She was walking that walk – the powerful, sexy one. The one that said 'I am in control'. Nick shoved his hands in his trouser pockets. His cock had begun to respond and he didn't want just anyone knowing about it. Alex Dumont had just come out of reception. And there was Jenna chatting to him, smiling and shaking her head. What had that girl been doing? She looked as if she'd been up all night.

Lisette thrust out her hand. 'Car keys.'

A little shiver went through Nick. God, she was sexy when she was ordering him about! But hey, he was Nick Treganza, the MD, the big man. It was one thing for her to dominate him once in a while in bed. But they needn't broadcast that little secret.

'Was hitting the old champers a bit hard last night,' he explained loudly to no one in particular in the gathering crowd, 'and my wife obviously reckons I'm still over the limit – bless her.'

That should do it, he thought as he handed over the keys. Cast Lisette back in the role of the businessman's supportive wife. But instantly she turned and handed the keys of Nick's precious Toyota Land Cruiser to Alex Dumont.

'Lisette,' Nick floundered, 'what's going on?'

She turned and looked at him hard. 'That's your company car. You drive it by virtue of your position as MD of the company whose name you changed to Treganza Leisure International. I'm still the majority shareholder, remember? I'm replacing you.

'Oh, I know we have to do it all officially. I'll call an Emergency General Meeting as soon as we're all back in London. But in practical terms consider yourself ... not sacked – demoted. You'll be needed for day to day management. Alex has no plans to move from Houston. He'll be the new MD. Did I mention that?'

Nick shivered despite the early sun's warmth on the back of his neck. This wasn't true. This was the worst thing that could possibly happen. And the audience was growing by the second.

'Lisette – why? I thought ... last night ... I thought things were good ...'

'I'm fed up, Nick. Not with your affairs. I knew when I married you you couldn't keep your cock buttoned up. Nor do I have any desire for a divorce. I'm fed up with being treated like a cash cow. It was my company first. You never give me any credit for that. I want control back.' She turned and grinned over her shoulder. 'And Alex knows very well I'm not going to let it go again.'

She took a step closer to Nick and whispered in his ear – though why she bothered with a whisper he couldn't guess as most of the hushed crowd could still hear her – 'Alex will be flying over once a month to keep tabs on the business. And he gets so bored of staying in hotels. Don't you, *chèri*? He'll be staying in our house, Nick. In our bed. And you will do exactly as you're told. And yes, you're right. Last night was good. But it's only the beginning . . .'

Nick was shaking. He hoped no one could see. This was a living hell. So how come part of him thought it was heaven, too?

Domination. Sexually. Career-wise. Submission was his last taboo. It all came together. He imagined himself looking on – a voyeur – as Alex Dumont, in Nick's own bed, turned his wife face down and penetrated her. He and Lisette had been having an affair all along? He was amazed to find the thought excited him.

'I'll leave you to think about that,' Lisette cut in. 'Or perhaps from the look on your face you already have. You see, I know you, Nick. Better than you know me. We'll see you in London.' Then she looked beyond him and smiled her over-sweet smile that always meant trouble. 'Jenna can give you a ride. In her car, I mean.'

She walked away – powerful, hips swinging – and eased into her buttercup-yellow sports car. Alex climbed into the four by four with a 'See you in London, pal.'

Nick wanted to grasp his creepy bald head and smash it against the windscreen. But . . . but . . . he wanted other things, too. Someone to master him.

The crowd began to ease away as if only Lisette's personality had held them there. A porter came up and coughed.

'Where would you like your luggage, sir?'

'Just dump it there,' Nick muttered.

There was a slam. He looked up. That tall, dark-bearded man had just jumped down from the back of the nearest white van and banged shut the other door. Now both doors were shut Nick could see the full logo.

>Robin Treganza
>Historical Re-enactments
>and Entertainments
>Unlimited

Christ, it couldn't be? There had been something niggling about him all weekend. It had been twenty years ... But of course it was. How many other Treganzas were there?

'Bobby,' he spat out. 'Bobby the brat. Meet my long-lost cousin, folks. With a sense of timing. Come to stick the knife in as well?'

'It's Robin these days. Hello, Nick. Wonder why I got the contract to run this weekend? I bid lower than anyone else. You being a cheapskate I knew you couldn't resist.'

'Seems a lot of bother to go to just to fuck up my party. People who hold a grudge that long need to get a life. Or did you just want a ringside seat?'

'I'm nothing to do with your wife's stunt. I didn't even know what was going on till Saturday night. Sure, I was out to make mischief. You were a bastard when we were kids. I doubt you've changed. Always trying to put someone else down to make yourself feel good.'

'What would you know? You were the one who came out of it okay. Took off with your parents and my dad and their hippy ideas. Me and Mum were the ones who got left. Called names by the neighbours. Hassled on the way to school. Don't you try making me feel guilty.'

'Way I heard it, your mum threw your dad out because she was so uptight. Couldn't cope with his libido. You're a lot like him, Nick. He works for me now, your old man. I'm just off to join him.' Robin held out his hand. Nick ignored it. 'Want me to pass on a message?' Nick shook his head. 'Sorry about what happened with your job. No, really I am. I confess I meant to make you look an idiot – for all the times you made me look stupid, made me feel small, when we were growing up. I didn't know things would go this far.'

Nick turned his back, damned if he was going to shake that man's hand. Not now. He looked at Jenna. Loyal Jenna. She'd waited on the drive while all the other guests had contracted acute embarrassment and sidled away.

'I notice Lisette didn't repossess *your* company car,' he snapped. 'You'd better drive me back.'

Jenna narrowed her eyes at him for a moment. Just for a split second he couldn't tell what she was thinking. Then she slapped her car keys into his hand.

'Drive yourself back to London. I've made other arrangements. I'll be in touch.'

She picked up her suitcase, pushed past him, opened the back door of Robin's van and tossed her luggage in.

Nick didn't wait. He didn't want to know. He grabbed his own bags, marched over to Jenna's car, let himself into the driving seat and screwed his eyes shut.

Images partied in his head. He was back home in their expensive designer bedroom: all Lisette's taste, of course. He was tied to a hard wooden chair. Naked. Leather straps were biting into his wrists behind his back. Maybe he was gagged. In his lap his cock was standing up straight.

Lisette and Alex were on the bed. Alex was thrusting his own cock proudly into Lisette. She was moaning and crying out for more. For Alex to go on for ever. She knew he could. She was worshipping his virility. Responding as Nick had never got her to respond. He was the lesser man.

Humiliation flooded over him like a warm shower. It was sweet. It pushed open a stuck door in his mind. In real life he felt his erection tightening in his pants. He began rifling through the case he'd dumped on the passenger seat. Where was Eleni's mobile number again?

Robin chuckled as he helped Jenna into the back of the van.

'So you've made "other arrangements"? News to me.'

'News to me, too. Just a spur-of-the-moment decision.'

'I approve of those.'

'Really . . . It's a shock. Him and Lisette. I had no idea she was going to do that. For a moment there I felt for him. Wanted to rush up and throw my arms round him and tell him everything would be okay. But then he tried to order me about. Expected me to jump like I've always jumped. That's what did it.'

'Everything will be okay. For Nick. He'll bounce back. He's always made the best of a situation – don't believe anything different.' He sighed and squeezed her shoulder. 'We've all laid a few ghosts this weekend. Stop smirking, Jenna! I'm glad it's over. We can get on with our lives now.'

Robin climbed into the van after her and shut the door. The redheaded twins were in the front seats. They turned and winked. One of them started the engine.

'We're headed totally the wrong way for London,' Robin continued as he settled himself on a pile of clothes. 'Next stop, Bodmin. Sure you want to stay on board?'

Jenna sat down beside him. The soft mass of theatrical costumes yielded under her weight. And they had that scent about them. That mossy, tingly, subversive scent. She breathed it in and held it.

'I'm exploring my options.'

'Another thing I approve of.'

The van swung as it took the curve of the long gravel drive. She was thrown against Robin. He took advantage of the movement and clasped her shoulder, keeping her body pressed against his. He began to kiss her on the mouth then worked his way down over her neck. They slipped down to horizontal on the cushions. He eased down the shoulders of her summer top and began running his tongue in circles down her cleavage at the edge of her lacy half-cup bra.

There was a movement in the front of the van. One twin unclipped her seat belt and clambered over the back of the passenger seat. She joined them on the spreading, spilling mass of velvet and brocade.

She'd wanted to do this for days. Jenna slipped her hand under the other woman's T-shirt and cupped her big, warm breast. It felt soft, welcoming. Robin moved round behind her. He lifted up her top and his tongue began working its magic circles all the way down the hollow of her spine, coming to rest in the sensitive small of her back. The movement of the van as it lumbered on to the main road rocked their three bodies together.

They began to strip off Jenna's clothes. Robin undid her skirt zip with his teeth and nibbled at the edge of her lace panties. The redhead pulled her top up over her head and began to fondle her breasts through her stiff, underwired bra. Jenna parted her legs and Robin began to kiss and mouth her bush through her panties. At the same time he began unzipping the other woman's jeans, delving in and finger-pleasuring her.

A complete circle, thought Jenna as she and the redhead unclipped each other's bras and pressed their yielding breasts together. They rolled each other's nipples, sighing with mutual rapture as their lips met in a deep French kiss.

This was so beautiful, so sharing, so inclusive, Jenna thought. It could go on for ever. And why not? There was plenty of time. London and the office could wait – till next week, or the week after . . . Or there was always Alex and America. Right now, as Robin eased down her panties and began probing her with his tongue, she couldn't imagine wanting to be anywhere else.